# Chapter One

It is early morning and I wake up to a familiar sound, the sound of multiple crinkles of plastic. I start to get excited in hopes it is what I think it is, my mom set out my favorite chocolate covered donuts. I sit up in my bed slowly and carefully, as I know if I sit up too quickly, I will surely hit my head on the beam of the ceiling yet again. I had a red metal bunk bed; it was my favorite bed. It didn't have a bottom bunk however, there was no need for one. I was an only child. My high sitting bed certainly did not fit well in our tiny, one-bedroom basement apartment in Napa, California. We were slightly below ground, with 4-foot doors. It was like a basement for hobbits, which was fitting for my mom and I. I loved our little place, it was home.

I had zero embarrassment or insecurities about our dark underground unit because it was all I knew. I was about four years old, and it was just my mom and me. Our little place was ours; I would often walk outside and walk up these stairs to this old woman's unit who lived alone. I would play cards with her for hours. I loved hanging out with her, she would sit in this old recliner with a vomit yellow colored knitted blanket. She had all sorts of knick-knacks and treasures in her house, and I loved it. She almost seemed like a witch but with a warm loving presence. I would often play make believe scenes by myself, I was a fairy, or a princess, and I would walk around this tiny back patio area pretending I was on a magical adventure.

I have very few memories of where we lived before. When my mom was still with my dad, we lived in a house, I had my own bedroom, with my awesome bunk bed. I remember the neighbors would throw their dirty diapers over the fence in our backyard and my mom would get furious and chuck them back. I remember my parents throwing big parties with tons of their friends, their kids, music, beer, smoking, and cocaine, these were just normal get togethers as it seemed. My grandparents, who were my dad's parents had this beautiful house in Napa with a pool. I loved going there, I would wear my grandmother's nightgowns and pretend I was a beautiful princess. My grandmother was a very beautiful, classy woman. Her hair was always perfect, and her clothing was like something out of a magazine. She was stunning to look at. My grandfather was an athletic man, a star athlete growing up and taught me how to play baseball. He would pitch to me and teach me how to swing a bat properly. One day he pitched to me, and I slugged the ball so hard it went right over the fence and disappeared. I dropped the bat in fear that I was going to get in trouble for losing the ball, when my grandpa jumped up and down and cheered. He was so proud of me. Our routine was we would play baseball, and then eat drumstick ice cream cones together. They were the best grandparents ever, but unfortunately as time went on, my grandfather had passed of cancer. My grandmother was a widow for years, until she too got sick and passed. Together, they were what true love looked like.

One night my mom and dad got in a fight. I remember my mom walking in the living room and slamming a little black book down on a table. It looked like a phone book of some sort. My mom shouts "I'm sick of this shit! Danny" It is clear now, that my dad had been caught cheating, yet again. This fight was the one that finally made her leave. I have blocked everything out from what happened after that until my memory flashes to me walking through our dark house, following my mom's cries. I slowly walked into the kitchen to see my mom, sitting on the floor with her face buried in her hands. "I just want my mom" she cried. My mom's mom, Jo had sadly passed away just a about a year prior. Leaving my mom and her brother without any parent at this point. Their dad was a drug dealer for the Hell's Angels and was found dead with a needle in his arm. They never had anything good to say about him as a father. My mom didn't care about him, but she cared about her mom. I, at the age of four, seeing my mom sad, broken, and alone, slowly put my hand on her knee to comfort her as she cried and said, "It's okay mommy."

# Chapter Two

My mom and I moved out after leaving my dad, and into our little basement apartment. My mom got me a pet bunny and I named him "Bugs." He looked just like Bugs from Looney Toons, but he was mean. He bit me all the time, but I love him still, he was so soft and my first pet. Before I knew it, my mom took me up to South Lake Tahoe, California. She was introducing me to her new boyfriend, Jed and his two kids, Jenny and Jax. Jenny was less than two years older than me, and Jax was less than two years younger than me. Jax was tall, dark, and handsome. He was of Armenian and Italian descent. You could tell that he was a man of confidence but in an intimidating way. He was a firefighter and has a nice big house in South Lake Tahoe. I have never seen a house so pretty, with an upstairs kitchen and a view of the mountains and a backyard view of the Lake.

Meeting Jenny and Jax was awkward to say the least. These two kids looking at me, and me looking back at them, all three of us slightly unaware of what this meant. Jenny had this beautiful strawberry blonde hair with green eyes. She had a light complexion and was very shy. Jax looked like his dad, darker complexion, light brown hair, with light brown eyes. It was odd to me how different they looked from each other, but they most definitely had the same mom and dad. Jenny looked just like her mom Rosie, a beautiful red head with a bright smile. I looked almost identical to my mom. We were both very petite with naturally long, thick dirty blonde hair, my mom's hair was lighter blonde and mine would brighten up in the summer with the sun. My mom, Tinsley had blueish- gray eyes and I had hazel. My dad, Danny was darker complected with dark brown eyes. In a way, I guess you could say my mom had a type.

I hardly even remember packing our things, or saying goodbye to that old woman I would play cards with. Within a blink of an eye it seemed, we moved to Tahoe and were officially living at my mom's new boyfriend's house. Jenny and Jax were back and forth between our house and their mom's house. I loved it when they came home, my new stepsister Jenny and I became close. I hated it when they would go back to their mom's, I would sit by the front door on the days I knew they were coming back. I loved feeling like I had a brother and a sister.

I was always jealous of my friends who had siblings. And here I finally felt like I could say that I have siblings.

Jenny, Jax, and I would ride bikes in our neighborhood, and organize big soccer games with the neighbor kids. We had a tree fort, and a lagoon we would fish at. Jenny and I shared a room, and we would have a special theme and color scheme as well. We loved to change it up here and there too. Jenny and Jax were both extremely picky eaters. They hated vegetables, and only liked the plainest of things. I loved vegetables and would sit there and watch them be repulsed by what their new stepmom would cook. I couldn't understand how someone could be disgusted by broccoli; it was delicious. My stepdad wouldn't let us be excused from the table unless our plates were clear. I personally wasn't a fan of pineapple, or Jed's only signature recipe… meatloaf. So, Jenny, Jax, and I would swap under the table when Jed and my mom weren't looking. I give them my pineapple as I ate their greens. We had quite the system.

When Jenny and Jax would go back to their mom's, I felt so lonely. Jed and his ex-wife Rosie were constantly fighting over custody in court. I would watch my mom sit and type paper after paper for Jed. They had an office full of papers, files, and boxes of nothing but court paperwork. Jed and Rosie did not have a civil divorce, and it seemed very toxic. He was either fighting for more or full custody, and it went on for years. We had a neighbor, Larry, who would come join us for dinner often. He was a wise, old man, full of stories and funny songs he would sing. He was short, stocky and full of personality. He was like a grandfather to me. Larry had a German shepherd named Tahoe. Tahoe was the greatest dog I had ever met. He would walk with Larry across the street and lay outside our front door waiting for him to be done at our house and then walk home with him when Larry was done.

Tahoe and I bonded, he loved me so much that when the school bus would drop me off at the bus stop, Tahoe was sitting there waiting for me. He would walk me home, and then walk back home to Larry's house. I loved him so much, and his love for me was very special. He wasn't like this with other kids in the neighborhood. One time, our neighbor friend Garrick wanted to see how loyal Tahoe was to me and he pretended to hit me, Tahoe chased him all the way home. I laughed so hard, he never tested him again. If we all went swimming in the lagoon, I would pretend like I was drowning and Tahoe would jump in the water, swim to me so I could hold on to his back, and swim me back to shore.

When Larry passed, I asked my mom and Jed if we could keep Tahoe. But unfortunately, Tahoe went to Larry's daughter who lived elsewhere. I was heartbroken. If Larry couldn't be here for Tahoe, then I was the next best option for him. His daughter didn't know or love Tahoe like I did. When Tahoe left that day with her, I was shattered. It made no sense, and I wish my mom and Jed would have at least asked. I almost wish I could have asked Larry himself before he passed. I know for a fact he would have wanted Tahoe to be with me when he passed. It was so hard to get off the bus and to not have Tahoe sitting there, waiting for me. I knew from here on out, German Shepherds will forever be my favorite dog.

## Chapter Three

The day my mom married Jeff was a funny memory for me. They got married in a cheap looking wedding chapel. The place looked like an old, A-frame cabin in South Lake Tahoe. It was my mom, Jed, Jenny, Jax, and myself, no other guests. They quickly got married, it probably took twenty minutes or so, and we all headed straight to Disney Land. I wanted to call Jed "dad" so badly. I didn't really see my real dad much once my mom and I moved into our hobbit house. So, I wanted Jed to be my dad, because I also wanted to feel like Jenny and Jax were even more like my brother and sister. For some reason, I felt as if I was not entirely welcomed as a part of the family.

On our drive to Disney Land. Jenny and I were sitting in the back of a van that my mom and Jed had rented. Jenny and I both had chocolate milk in our hands and we each had a barbie. I loved barbies, I couldn't get enough of them. It was beyond Barbie being so beautiful, it was about this "life" that I would create for her in my head. A good family, beautiful, a cute pet dog, handsome Ken, etc. It was this beautiful vision I would have in my head and only I got to design it. No one else. I would spend hours "setting up" an entire day in the life of Barbie when I would play.

Jenny and I became pretty competitive at times and as we were in the van, she and I got in an argument about whose barbie was prettier. Then I threw chocolate milk on her barbie, and Jenny got me good by pouring chocolate milk on me. My stepdad pulled the van over and had us get out on the side of the freeway to fight it out. We screamed and scratched and spit. Looking back on this memory makes the two of us laugh to this day. Although, at the time, this was only about forty-five minutes into us legally being stepsisters.

Once we got to Disney Land I started to pick up on things. My stepdad Jed would almost make it obvious that I wasn't his kid. And Jax was starting to make comments like "well you're not our real sister." Although he was right, it hurt. I hated how that made me feel. I hated feeling like I didn't belong in "their" house, and that I had no dad. My dad would keep in touch here and there throughout the years and send Christmas presents, but it wasn't the same. We weren't close. My mom told him that if he dared fight for custody then she would turn him and all his friends in for being drug dealers.

I wanted to belong to my current household so badly that I would dread if someone ever asked, "are you all siblings?" because then I knew Jed or Jax would make it very clear that I wasn't fully his kid or their sister. I always hoped that if someone were to ask if they were my siblings that they would only ask me in private so I could say "yes."

A couple years or so went by and my mom was pregnant. I was eight years old now I was officially going to be a big sister to a baby girl where we would both have the same mom. I was so excited for this moment. And then, my mom got pregnant almost immediately after having my baby sister Caley. She gave birth to a baby boy, Tyler. I was now a sister to two siblings. Even though we had different dads, I did not care. I felt as if they were my real siblings. Caley was also spelt with a "C" which made me so happy because my name was with a "C" as well, Candi.

Things changed drastically after my mom had my brother and my sister. My stepdad was working at the fire station a lot, he would work about forty-eight hours straight then have four days off. My mom was left to do a lot on her own. Including taking care of Jenny and Jax while they were with us. We had five kids total in our household and it was busy. My mom also worked full time at our local hospital in the finance department. But I was starting to realize I wasn't really treated the same, even by my own mom.

Caley and Tyler were so close in age that people would often mistake them as twins. My mom was so proud to have her new family. The firefighter husband, the house, the beautiful kids, but then there was me. We would always have a sit-down dinner, and for some reason, my stepdad would make me the only one who had to clear the table and do the dishes. There were times we would all have to pitch in with the clearing, but it wasn't every time for Jenny and Jax as it was for me. Or Jed would give them the easy task of drying plates while I did the brunt of the work. Jed would do this simple mind trick of why he always asked me to do the chores, he would say "because you're the best at it." I strived for this compliment. I was damn good at cleaning, because I was so desperate for the recognition. It would be little things like if my stepdad had to saw a piece of wood in the garage, he would walk up the stairs to Jenny, Jax, and I watching TV or playing and he would say "Candi, go vacuum up the sawdust in the garage." And with as many kids as we had in our house. The laundry was always piled up, and I had to do it. I would fold it and put it away and it was never ending. Jed got a little smarter with how he would get away with making me do all the work throughout the house, he would say it was to work off "time" from being grounded. I was always grounded. He was the punisher, and I was always in trouble. It was hard for me to understand because I wasn't a bad kid, I had developed an attitude because I was becoming resentful of what my life was like and my mom allowing it. I would talk back and then get "grounded" so I had to do more work to earn this "time off." However, there were times I knew I couldn't dodge being punished, Jed would find a way and it was clear.

# Chapter Four

I was beginning to struggle. I was about nine years old, and I was still peeing the bed. Since I was little, I had always wet the bed. It was so hard for me, and so embarrassing that I still needed to be in pull-ups. I would decline any and all sleepovers with my friends because I didn't want them to know that I had this ridiculous crunchy diaper I had to wear. I was also pulling out my eyelashes. I don't know what it was, but I would pull them out. A form of self-mutilation that I knew nothing about. I am unsure as to why I did it. If I looked at my eyelashes and saw that they didn't look even, I would yank them out. And then I'd continue and continue until I hardly had anything left. I would pick and pick at things on my skin. For some reason in my head, I felt as if it was the only thing that I could control. I would obsessively pick if I felt that wasn't "looking" or "going" right with me.

Things at home weren't going well. I had a daily reminder from my stepdad that I was not his kid. I was the only one in the household with a different last name. I hated how excluded I felt that I so badly wanted to legally change my last name to be the same as theirs, in hopes to feel a part of the family. Seeing as my mom and stepdad now had two kids together, it seemed as if he got more comfortable with how he could mistreat me. I don't ever remember my mom and Jed being loving or affectionate, they always fought, argued, and she was always angry, but she would never compromise her new family.

My mom also had a very bad temper. It didn't really matter who was watching, if she was angry, she would show it. I was also jealous of my friend's moms who never showed their crazy. And if they had it, they would at least hide it when their friends were around and do it behind closed doors. My mom did not care. If she was mad, she would show it. Even when I was younger, if I made her mad, she would pull down my pants in front of everyone at the grocery store and spank my bare bottom hard. The spanking wasn't the issue, kids get spankings all the time, it was the public humiliation that I hated. I still have vivid memories of me turning bright red with embarrassment as people would be mortified at the sight of it. I hate scenes to this day, I panic at the thought of an audience witnessing something so embarrassing and personal. Sometimes I wished she'd just take me to the bathroom like other parent's would threaten. But not my mom, when she was mad, she had no gage.

One day before school, I was in the sixth grade. My mom and I were in her car outside of school. She was trying to put my hair up and brushing it hard. She would rip through my hair as if a knot in my hair was at fault. She would yank it out of annoyance, and my head would jerk back, then she'd shove my head forward if I moved. I would squeal in pain which further angered her. She did one final rip right through my hair and I said "OWWW!" Before I knew it, I could hear an increasing wind like sound on my right side. SMACK! My mom had taken the flat backside part of the brush and smacked my face with it. I'll never forget how bad it stung, my eyes huge with shock, and worst of all… My mom, with no remorse. She continued with my hair, and I didn't make a peep. With tears slowly running down my face, I didn't want to even sniffle out of fear it would happen again.

My stepdad would get so angry with me over the smallest things that it quickly turned physical. I was small for my age, and he was about six feet. He would get into a fit of rage and grab me from behind the neck and lift me off the ground. The grab of the neck was so strong that it would pull my skin so tight that I couldn't breathe. Feeling my feet dangle off the ground was a weekly occurrence. He would pick me up by my neck and throw me down the first landing of the stairs at times. He was smart; however, he would never punch or do anything that would leave a mark. He was a firefighter and knew exactly what he was doing.

When I was twelve my dad moved to from Napa to Colorado. My mom took me to the airport to get on a plane to go visit him for the first time for about a week. I had never been on an airplane before and I was so excited to get away from my stepdad that I couldn't wait to fly to see what felt like a stranger to me, my dad. My mom was nice enough to take me to Claire's to get my second earring holes pierced before I got on the plane. I loved that she let me get my second piercing, but I see now that it was her way of making sure I knew I had a "good life" to return to after that week of visiting my dad.

Seeing my dad was innocuous. It was great to spend time with him, but it wasn't this outstanding father daughter time. We did play baseball which was always my favorite to play with him as it was mine and my grandfather's thing. I loved his dog Judd. Judd was a German Shepherd lab mix. He was the sweetest boy ever and I loved dogs so much. The week went by fast, and I didn't want to go back home. I missed my mom because I was more comfortable with her, but I hated everything else.

I hated my life. I hated my stepdad so much but hated my mom more for witnessing what my stepdad was doing to me for years. She never did anything about it. One time my stepdad got furious with Jax this time and did the same thing to him. Jax told his real mom, Rosie about it and CPS was called to our house. I had to lie to CPS that day when they questioned me about the things Jed would do when he was angry. My mom told me if I told CPS what he did then we would have nowhere to live, and our lives would be ruined. I hated that day, I felt as if this was my only chance to get away from him and then Caley, Tyler, and I could live a better life with my mom. But I lied, I lied for my mom.

I found myself fantasizing about ways for him to die. I knew that my mom would never leave him, so he would just have to die. I would think about how maybe if I caught a bunch of black widows and put it in his bed then they'd bite him, and he'd die. And then I realized that would put my mom and everyone else at risk too. So, I ignored that fantasy. When he would go to work, I would run upstairs and spit into his sock drawer. I hated him, I hated him so much. I couldn't believe that my life was coming to this point, as being only twelve years old and wanting someone to die. And I swore to myself that he could hit me as much as he wanted, but if he hit my mom then I would hit him back one day. I was always listening to their fights for my moment to come in and save her. I almost prayed that would happen because then, just then maybe if he hit her then she'd finally have enough, and if I saved her then she would love me more. But he never hit her, it was just me.

I was so angry inside, and no one knew it because I never showed it in my social life. I loved my friends, I loved animals, but if someone was mean to me, I would defend myself. I had a smart mouth, and I would always stand up for myself. Many of my friends found it amazing how I was quick to stand up for myself or others, but it was my defense mechanism. I knew all I had was my voice. I was in this constant fight or flight mode. I showed this on the soccer field as well. It was like I was easily triggered by bullies. I was never innocent people; it was mean people. I didn't care how small I was, I was unafraid to speak up.

## Chapter Five

When I was fourteen for Christmas Jed got me a dog. It was the best day of my life. I went with him to pick out the puppy at this breeder's house in El Dorado Hills, CA. She was my world, a German Shepherd, I named her JoJo. I have never loved anything so much in my life. And I for once, couldn't wait to come home from school to see her. My stepdad made her sleep in the garage at first, and I would sneak out there in the middle of the night to sit with her. Jed caught me, then grounded me, which resulted in another neck grab, and more chores.

Although Jed had this vicious cycle with me, we, as a family still did things together. We would go camping, we would have water fights, big birthday parties for Caley and Tyler, with a rented bouncy house, a paddle boat that we would take around the lagoon and go fishing, squirt gun fights, etc. I played soccer and I was in Taekwondo. Jed loved martial arts and he would work with me on my form. This was the one thing that made me feel like we had a bond. He knew I was good at Karate, and he was impressed. We had some beautiful times that were happy, and even though I was treated differently at times, I cherished those moments.

Jed was building a new home for us; he bought a lot and was doing a lot of the work himself to save money. Which is where I came in handy. He would make me sand, paint, pop out tile spacers, all sorts of things to "earn time off" being grounded. This is where he would justify why Jenny and Jax got to stay home with my mom and the babies and I had to be at the new house and work with him, because I, of course was grounded. It didn't matter if it was a school night or not, if there was work, there I was. He would find reasons ground me; I couldn't catch a break from punishment for the life of me. It was a sure way to make sure I was sentenced to certain chores.

In school I was the class clown. I loved making people laugh; I loved being the entertainer. Many people say kids are shyer at school and more comfortable at home, whereas I was the opposite. My personality shined outside of my home. I wasn't celebrated much at home; like I was at school. People would tell me daily that I should be an actress one day. I could do impressions of anything and turn anything into comedy. I loved making people laugh. I was athletic, and good at sports. Soccer was my all-time favorite, I played soccer my whole life. I also loved boys, I was boy crazy and always had a crush on someone. I would often jump from boyfriend to boyfriend. I preferred some sort of connection and attention because I hated my home life. I looked forward to just staying in my room and writing letters or talking on the phone to my friend's and boyfriend at the time. My mom was always so busy with the babies that it allowed me to just constantly care about my social life.

My freshman year was a life changing year for me. I was an amazing soccer player, I was Homecoming Princess, and a senior was taking interest in me. Jose Medina, he was a "bad boy." Like a wannabe gangster. He rode this low rider bike with a speaker in the back, and my friend Brittany had a thing for his friend Hector. The two of us blonde freshman girls would stand by our locker and get so giddy when Jose and Hector would walk by. Once they both gave us attention it was like fire. Brittany's parents weren't as strict as mine, so after school her mom would let the boys come over and hang out with us.

We would all sit in Brittany's room and make-out nonstop with our senior "bad boys." I was crazy for him. The boys would bring alcohol over and that's when I got drunk for the first time. Jose would always feed me shot after shot then try and tell me it was "time" for us to have sex for the first time. He would say things like "you're ready." And almost put it in my head that I was in fact "ready."

I waited a few weeks, when my mom and Jed allowed him to come over as I babysat Caley and Tyler. My mom and Jed had tickets to the Wayne Brady show, so they were going to be gone for a few hours. Jose and I went into the smallest bathroom of our house, where it could only fit a sink and a toilet. We started kissing and I finally allowed it to happen. I was nervous, and only doing it as a favor to him. The pain was almost unbearable, it hurt so bad I had no idea why anyone would enjoy this.

Afterwards, I was emotional. I was unsure of what this meant and what my friends would all think. Brittany was still a virgin; all my friends were actually; I was the only one who wasn't. About three weeks had gone by and I was now regularly having sex with Jose. We were completely unsafe. We never used a condom, the only "sexual education" I received in school was that I was going to start my period one day. I was terrified I was pregnant; it was the month of February, and I was young, I had barely started my period that year and I didn't get my period that month.

I called my stepsister Jenny who was at her mom's house to ask for help. She had her license, so I figured the next time she was up to stay with us, she could take me to get a test, or an abortion of I needed it. I was terrified. I told Jose I was scared, and he was almost excited. As if he wanted to have babies with me. I wasn't ready for that. I never wanted to be a mom, I saw how my mom was and how she wasn't loving and nurturing. I had no example of what a beautiful home life was like, so I despised the thought of it. I called up Jenny and said, "Jenny, I don't know what to do, I think I am pregnant. I need help."

Chapter Six

My alarm goes off and I start to get up and get ready for school as I always do. I picked out a pair of my favorite bell bottoms and my favorite belt. I finished putting on a little mascara as I walked across my room to grab a bracelet. It was early, about 7:15am when my stepdad opens my bedroom door and says, "Where do you think you're going?" I look at him with complete and utter confusion and said, "to school?" He had a smirk on his face, almost like he was excited for something. He said, "come upstairs." I slowly follow him upstairs where my mom is sitting on the couch. Jed sits next to her as I sat on the other couch confused. My mom then says, "Did you have sex with Jose?" I immediately lied and said "No!" My mom then replies, "Do you swear to God?" Although we weren't very religious, and we never went to church, something deep within me always valued never lying on God's name. I was never raised to value this, but it was an expectation that I had for myself. I looked down at my hands and quietly said. "No…." as in no, I don't swear to God. That was my confession, then and there my life changed forever.

My stepdad looked at me and said, "you have two choices, you can either go to a girl's home in Utah or go live with your mom's friend Sandy in Napa." The fact that those were my only two choices made me sick. I opted for Napa but disgusted that this was my only destiny. I was angry with Jenny for telling on me. My stepdad told me to go downstairs and pack my things. That's when my jaw hit the floor, "now?" I asked. "Now." He spoke. I wasn't even allowed to go to school. I wasn't even allowed to call my best friends to tell them I had to move... today!

I was packing my things, in tears. My mom left for work. As my stepdad and I loaded my things into his truck for our three-hour drive ahead of us. The fact that my mom, my own mom, was making me move... for losing my virginity. My stepdad and I got in the truck and I couldn't even look at him. I kept thinking about jumping out of the car while it was moving, wanting to call my friends, or even my boyfriend to let them know I was leaving, for good.

We stopped at the doctor's office on the way out of town. He put in the truck in park when I looked up at my stepdad and asked, "What are we doing?" "You're going to get a checkup" he said. Before I knew it, I had a speculum inside me, swab after swab, and a blood draw. I was beside myself I could barely breathe. We stopped by my mom's office after. I walked into her office, and I looked at her as she sat at her desk and said, "Mom why are you doing this?" with tears in my eyes. I wasn't mad, I was sad. My whole life I've been mad, extremely mad. Mad at my stepdad, mad at her, mad. But right now, right now, I was sad. I was so sad. This level of pain, rejection and loneliness, was unbearable. How could she just dispose of me like this? Just get rid of me like this.

On the drive down Jed and I didn't speak. He almost had a smile on his face. He was happy he had won; he was happy he was getting rid of me. He had his wife, his two kids, and his other two kids whom he loved. I was the one who didn't belong, I was not wanted there, not by him or her. I couldn't even bring my dog. I had to say goodbye to JoJo, which hurt me most. I kept thinking of ways to kill myself. I kept thinking about the time I wrote in a diary about all the times Jed had been violent towards me and then I threw the whole diary in the lagoon because I knew no one would ever save me. Everything was flashing before my eyes. I hated Jed, I hated my mom.

## Chapter Seven

A few months had gone by and living at Sandy's house wasn't easy either. I was under close watch there. I wasn't allowed to use the phone to call my friends there either. No one knew where I went. I went from an amazing soccer player, homecoming princess, and class clown to a disappearance. From time to time, I'd try to sneak a call in to finally get ahold of my friends to tell them where I was, and that's when Brittany told me my mom showed up at school and in front of everyone, pulled her out of class to get her to open our locker so my mom could retrieve my schoolbooks. I was humiliated. Then she told me the rumors being spread about me. People were saying that I was pregnant and had to get an abortion, which thank God wasn't true. People were saying my stepdad walked in on me during sex, that I was on drugs, etc. The rumors made me even more angry because I could have at least prevented that if I was at least given a chance to say goodbye to my friends and explain why. I didn't even care if everyone knew I was no longer a virgin, the rumors were far worse at this point.

Being the new girl at a public school toward the last quarter of the year wasn't easy either. Luckily, I had two cousins that went to that high school so that was reassuring. But they were older and had their friends, and cars, and I was under close watch so I couldn't get away with going off and doing whatever I wanted. After the school year had ended, I was finally allowed to move back home. I was so excited to come back, but also so scared to face everyone knowing these rumors about me were so absurd. When I moved back, I was still under major restriction. I had been living back at home for only about four days when the doorbell rang… It was Jose. I was shocked to see him. He walked all the way to my house which was extremely far from where he lived. I walked outside and felt nothing, I was over him. I hated my life, I hated that he convinced me I was ready to lose my virginity, I hate that he could've got me pregnant and enjoyed the thought of it when I was the one who was stressed about it. I had to move for God's sakes. But I then realized, he loved me. We were young and didn't know much else about life at that point. He loved me and wanted to be with me. And I loved him but didn't want my life to turn upside down like it did. I looked at him and said, "I don't know what to tell you, I'm over you." I had no choice. Although I wanted to say, "I missed you." I knew my only chance at freedom and never losing the roof over my head again was to keep him the hell away from me. This was for his safety and mine, I had to be cold. It killed me to see the look on his face. He walked away slowly, and we never spoke again.

I had called one of my friends that I hadn't seen since I moved because my mom and Jed were going to finally let me go to the movies. I called Andrea and invited her to come with me. She put the phone down to ask her mom. She didn't know it, but I could hear her mom's answer. She said, "No Andrea, I told you I don't want you hanging out with her." Andrea gets back on the phone and says, "Candi, my mom said no." I was embarrassed. I was this girl with some Scarlett letter on me in this town. After these rumors were spread, this wasn't the first time my friend's parents wouldn't let them hang out with me, it was numerous occasions.

When I was finally able to find a friend that was allowed to go with me, we get to the ticket stand. A girl from school that I knew came up to me and smacks my arm and says "Candi! You did crystal meth?" I looked at her confused and said, "Crystal Meth? Who is Crystal Meth? I've never even met her." My friend replied, "The drug?" I was so confused. I didn't even know what that was, and here was yet another rumor about me. I felt like I couldn't win. But I was happy to home.

Chapter Eight

    Living back at home was not as if my mom had missed me by any means. I was constantly walking on eggshells. My mom and Jed fought like crazy, and he was even more comfortable with being physically abusive towards me again considering he knew where her loyalty lied, it was with him. He had convinced her to make me move, and that was power to him. My mom had me start seeing a therapist. She even suggested that my stepdad see the same one. It was quite comical now to see how Jed would either put it in my head that no one was in my corner or if he had convinced people to think the worst about me. My stepdad told me out of anger that even the therapist didn't believe me and that I was a "liar." This accusation was probably the first time anyone has ever hurt my feelings with their words. I couldn't believe my own therapist would say that. After all I have done is tell my therapist what was going on in my life, my real life. This hurt me so badly. I felt betrayed, by my own therapist. I had a session with him, and I told the therapist what my stepdad said. I told him how ridiculous it was to say such a thing about me when all I've done is tell the truth. I couldn't even lie the day my life was essentially going to be over when I had to pack my things and move for losing my virginity. If I had lied that day, I wouldn't have had to go through all of that, but I refused. That was bullshit. My entire life I have been stripped of everything, and the one thing that I valued, that no one could take from me was my word. I didn't care if telling a lie made me look better or worse, I couldn't do it. I felt sick talking to my therapist about this. My therapist took one look at me and said, "Candi, I never said I don't believe you. And what your stepdad is doing to you is abuse." I was so taken back by his validation that I had no words. I couldn't even continue the session because I didn't want Jed to now get arrested. I hated him but didn't.

One night Jed and I got in a big argument. He lost all control and grabbed my neck and threw me. I started to run down the stairs and bravely said, "Don't you ever touch me again." He then chased after my and grabbed the back of my neck and forced me to the ground. I still remember the feeling of the cold tile on my forearms as I was pinned to the ground knowing it was about to get much worse. Before I knew it, my mom ran down the stairs and intercepted the altercation. I'll never forget the look on his face, he was shocked. I have never seen his eyes so huge in my life. We left that night and my mom and I got a hotel with my younger brother and sister that night. I begged my mom to let me bring JoJo my dog with me. I didn't want to leave her. JoJo was my everything. She followed me everywhere, and I would rather sleep under the same roof with Jed than to be without her.

I had hoped things were going to be better after this and that my mom was finally going to leave him. We were living in the new house that we built by then so technically we had two homes. I was hoping Jed could live in his first house and he would leave the new house to us. His first house was much bigger, his castle, and he planned to remodel it. So, I prayed that was going to be their arrangement. But it wasn't, we were back home the very next day.

Another argument followed a few weeks later between Jed and me. This time he told me to pack my things because they were going to make me move back to Napa. I was shaking, I couldn't go through this again. I looked at my mom in utter disbelief. I screamed, I screamed loudly and said, "How could you do this to me!" I ran downstairs and quickly opened the door that goes to the garage to get my dog to hug her. I opened the door so fast and in such a panic that it ripped right over my foot. Slicing a deep cut at the top of it. My emotions were at an all-time high I didn't even feel it. I sat on the back porch holding my dog and crying as my foot bled. I didn't want to move. All because of an argument, because I talked back, I had to move again. My siblings would get away with saying the same things, sometimes worse because they knew they would get away with it. But I was the family reject, I didn't have a comfortable, guaranteed spot in the house.

When I hear about kids getting kicked out of their parent's house, it is because it is often truly necessary. They either got into drugs, or were constantly in trouble with the police, or running away, or stealing from their parents. I didn't feel as if I was such a terrible kid to deserve this. Sure, I lost my virginity at a young age, and was finally starting to talk back here and there, but I wasn't a monster. My mom and Jed put it in my head that I had an attitude problem, so it justified any and all punishment, but looking back on it, I wasn't as bad as they painted me out to be. If my mom was on some sort of tirade and she would scream at me, it wasn't like a normal parent yelling at their kid, it was an obsessive high she would get from it. It could be the smallest thing, and if I were to respond by saying, "okay" in a snooty tone, it was almost as if she was hoping it would happen so she could unleash all this built-up anger and take it out on me.

My mom didn't end up making me move, but I of course was grounded as usual. It was less of a punishment thing and more of a way that if my stepdad knew I had a school dance coming or some sort of event coming up, he'd find a way to make sure I couldn't go to it. He knew I was popular and well liked outside of my home and knew he could compromise that. I was angry that he would even use the words "Pack your things" as a threat, whether he meant it or not, he knew how much it triggered me, and my mom allowed it.

## Chapter Nine

As it got closer to my sixteenth birthday, I ended up dating a new boy in my grade, Cody. He was the hottest boy in school. He looked like Stephen Colletti from Laguna Beach. A show that the girls my age were obsessed with at the time. He was around often; he was allowed to hang out when my mom was home, and I was allowed to go to his house. I loved his mom; she was a hard-working single mom with a big heart. I had soccer practice one day and Cody was driving with my mom to pick me up. My mom like I said, doesn't care who is around if something or someone makes her mad, she won't wait to react if there is an audience. She was yelling in the car at my brother and sister about something, when she looked over at Cody who was looking at her in shock. "What?" She sternly asked him. Cody replied and said, "Tinsley, do you like… like to yell?" This sent her over the edge. She was furious when she picked me up from soccer and told me, and then he wasn't allowed to come over for a while. She said he was beyond disrespectful. Cody had been around my family for months, and he certainly witnessed how my mom operated. I didn't really have him over when my stepdad was home, but he was over often when my stepdad was at the Fire Station.

One night I was sitting on the couch angry yet again about my stepdad and how my mom lets him treat me so differently. I didn't understand it. It's like my siblings could all say the same things as me, but only I would get in trouble. I always said how I wanted to go live with my dad. My mom sat me down one night while Jed was at the fire station and said, "Candi, I think your dad might have molested you when you were younger." I stopped; my stomach dropped. I burst into tears. I have very little memory of when I was much younger, but I don't remember anything like that happening. Did I block it out? Did he? I was so confused that I didn't know what to believe. I did have a rash in between my thighs for a while because I always peed myself, it was itchy and painful, and I remember my dad asked me about it, but I never remember him doing anything inappropriate to me. He was genuinely concerned about this rash, and now my mind was wondering if I had blocked something out. All I could do was cry; I truly believe he was only looking at the rash. Because there was a rash! I was so confused. And I felt like this was the first time my mom ever showed she had sympathy for me. My mom called him and told him that "I remember things." But she was clearly teeing off the rash memory I had.

The next day my dad called my cell phone and left me a message. He was furious. He said "Candi, I don't know what the fuck your mom is doing but she said I fucking molested you? She is a fucking nasty fucking cunt." That voicemail haunts me to this day. He was furious and I hated that word "molested." I never called him back. I didn't know what to say. I didn't know what to think.

I continued with therapy with a new therapist, but my therapy wasn't about my dad when I was in there. I wanted to talk about my stepdad and the continued dynamic that was unchanged in my household. Finally, I told my therapist everything about my stepdad, and how my stepdad told me it wasn't considered "abuse," he would simply say "I have the right to restrain you." That was bizarre, because I feared him, what do he so badly need to restrain? I had it in my head that the only thing that classifies abuse is punching, kicking, or hitting someone with objects, so I started to believe that I wasn't being truly abused. My therapist finally said in a firm tone. "Candi. What he is doing to you IS abuse." Boom, that was all I needed to hear. I needed for once someone else to at least confirm that is what it was called. For so long it was put in my head that this "wasn't abuse," grabbing me behind the neck and picking me up like that "wasn't abuse." I felt so relieved, not as if this meant it was never going to happen again. But that someone for once was agreeing that this was not okay.

Days later, my stepdad and I had a talk. He had this way about him where he was a toxic control freak and had a temper, but also very wise. I found myself admiring him in some ways. He would often share very insightful quotes about mastering your mindset that I enjoyed hearing. I hated how mean and controlling he was, but he was also inspiring in a way. We sat in his office; he sat in this wooden chair that he could lean back in. I had the courage to calmly tell him that my therapist said what he was doing to me was considered abuse. I started to cry, and then he started to cry. I was taken back by the emotion this man was showing. I had only seen him cry once when his mom passed away. But this? This was new. And he meant it. He hugged me, and said, "I'm sorry." Nothing more was needed to be said. I'll never forget that day. We still had our issues, and he would still have an outburst here and there, but it was becoming less and less. I started to notice we had less issues because he wasn't around as much. My mom and Jed were back and forth with each other. For years he had been going on trips out of town and often out of the country with his Fire fighter friends, and it bothered my mom. She knew he was most likely cheating. He would stay at his main house majority of the time, and said he was "working on the remodel." Then at times, he would stay with us at our other house. My mom loved him and stuck with it, it was always a fight with them, but I loved the fact that he wasn't around as much. My mom was so wrapped up in her golden children that I was just pretty much on my own. She was always angry, always on a mood, and I was walking on eggshells constantly. I stayed as busy as possible, I worked, played soccer, and then I got a new job as a hostess at a restaurant in the Marina close to my house.

By now I officially had my driver's license and was driving my mom's old red Toyota 4-runner. It was a stick shift, Jed taught me how to drive it. Hardly any of the boys at school knew how to drive a stick. This was another thing I was grateful for. The rules were, if I wanted to drive, then I needed to work to pay for my gas and car insurance. So, I did. Being a hostess wasn't my first job, but it was my first official apply and interview big girl job. I had worked in a clothing store before that was owned by a family friend. I loved it, I would ride my bike to work, and offered to work the entire ten hours because I loved it so much. I loved making my own money, I loved being around people. I loved people thanking me for helping them, it was so stimulating, it gave me such purpose.

Chapter Ten

Working at my new job gave me this new excitement in life. I was sixteen and working with a bunch of twenty something year old's who all loved to party. They treated me as if I was as old as they were. I had broken up with Cody because he was extremely jealous and insecure. It started to become draining. I broke his heart, but I communicated everything respectfully. He was a great guy but had some issues himself he needed to work through. I was checked out of anything that had to do with high school mentally. Then, there was a sushi chef who worked there caught my eye, Matt. Matt was twenty-six years old, dark brown hair and these big green eyes and he was very flirtatious. I was still in high school and officially had a crush on someone much older. My friends and I would go to his house and party and drink all the time. I hardly cared about school anymore, I lost focus in soccer, and it was obvious. I wasn't playing like I used to, I was sloppy, careless and don't even know what came over me anymore. Even my coaches were shocked. I had just let myself go, all I cared about was this older guy who gave me all this attention and wanting any sort of distraction away from home whether positive or negative.

After a while, Matt and I became more and more serious. I was finding ways to stay the night at his house by telling my mom I was staying at a friend's house. I would do anything to be with him. I was so scared to tell my mom the truth about him because of our age difference. But for some reason, even if I wasn't asked directly, I knew I couldn't live a lie. Matt didn't want to fully commit to me because of our age difference. I was desperate to convince him it was okay. I found myself getting jealous of the women I worked with who are all old enough to go to the bars with Matt after work. I had to stay home and go to school the next day while all my cool coworkers flirted with my secret boyfriend and doing God knows what. Matt was outgoing, a flirt, and girls flocked to him.

It came time for me to finally tell my mom. I felt like although my mom and I didn't have the most loving relationship, we were able to coexist better because Jed wasn't around as much. My mom was trying to make their marriage work, but he was working so much and always staying at the other house. Therefore, I felt as if my household was less strict. I finally said something, I was in my bedroom and my mom was in there with me. "I need to tell you something." I said nervously, with my hands on my head as if I had just got the wind knocked out of me. My mom knew I was hanging out with Matt, but she did not know how old he was. "What is it?" she asked. "It's about Matt, mom." She seemed calm, and said, "okay…?" I was sick, I felt as if it was going to be hell that froze over after I told her the truth. My mom proceeds to ask some heavy questions that made my confession seem like a piece of cake. "Did he rob a bank?" my mom asked. "What!? No." I shrieked. "Did he kill someone?" she asked. "Mom, what? No!" I snapped. "Then what is it?" she asked. "He's twenty-six." My stomach dropped. There it was, there was the truth. I couldn't feel like I was hiding this secret any further. My mom sighed and to my surprise, was very calm. "Well, I think you're very mature for your age." She said. I think that might have been the very first compliment she has ever given me. I couldn't believe how mellow she was about it. And we didn't really talk much further about it. It seemed so easy, and too good to be true.

I felt so much relief and immediately called Matt. "Hey!" I said excitedly when he answered the phone. "Hey…" he replied in a chill tone. "I told my mom about us. And she was fine with it!" I said. He was happy too, but in a mellow way. I truly don't think he was all that excited to be honest because he didn't really want to stop having all the hookups, he was having with all the girls at work. My age was an easy excuse for him to not want to commit to me. I knew he was probably sleeping with a few of our coworkers, it was like deep down I knew it was happening but didn't want to admit it to myself. I was weak, smitten, almost mesmerized by him. And to him, this was almost pressure on him because deep down he knew I wanted us to be more serious. He liked me but didn't want to be off the market.

I was stressing out about not knowing what he was up to most nights. Although my mom knew I was seeing him, he was not MY boyfriend, and not locked down by any means. I had a curfew, and school five days a week and he was going out to the casinos and bars with my coworkers. I was going crazy with insecurity. I was this guaranteed high school girl who was dumb enough to come to him whenever he snapped his fingers. How easy it was for him to have his cake and eat it too.

Things at home weren't mellow by any means. My mom was increasingly angry, and seemingly only towards me, it was almost as if she blamed me for her marriage not going well with Jed. How was it that I had been his punching bag for years and lied to CPS to "save" our family, yet I was to blame for everything? I almost regretted daily for never telling that social worker the truth. My mom always had a temper. Ever since I could remember, she was notorious for minor things, but they stood out to me. She would always slam doors, and yell. Even if we were in the car together, when I would sit in the passenger seat, if my head was blocking her vision while she was trying to look to the right, she would grab my head and slam it to the back of the seat. She made it clear that everything I did pissed her off. She was always disorganized, and lost her keys, and her credit cards almost daily. When she would rip apart her car, her purse, or the house to find them she did it with anger. When I would help her find whatever was missing, she would snap at me if I asked a simple question that might encourage me to look in a different location. It was like she would take it all out on me. I am extremely organized to this day, almost to an unhealthy level because I despise how chaotic and angry my mom was.

I couldn't stand how much my mom made me feel like she didn't want me around. Sure, she provided for me when I was younger. I had nice clothes, and she gave me her old car. But she reminded me of that daily. She provided for me while we were living with Jed full time. But every single thing she has ever done for me was used against me later. As if I had no right to have any sort of opinion or feeling about anything. I despise gifts or nice gestures to this day because I am so traumatized into thinking that if someone does something nice for me, then they get a hall pass to be cruel to me or take it away. Everything came with a price. She would put it in my head daily that I was spoiled rotten, and that I was ungrateful. I couldn't wrap my brain around this mentality because when I was little, we were so poor, so poor I didn't even know there was an alternative way of living. We had nothing, and I was happy. I liked my bunny, and I liked my bed. That is all I knew, and now because my mom bought me an Abercrombie and Fitch shirt, I was an consider a selfish, ungrateful, monster.

I never felt as if I was above working, I loved it. I loved the fact that I had to get a job, I loved any chance to be recognized and complimented on my hard work and efficiency. No one taught me how to be bubbly, outgoing, or how to have a work ethic. I did, I did that; on my own. My mom could never take credit for my personality or my work ethic. She was never warm and fuzzy to people; she was cold and short with others. So much so, that I found myself highly embarrassed for the way she would talk to anybody. I would almost exhaust myself trying to be extra kind to the people my mom encountered with me around.

I feel as if this is why I am overly affectionate with people and go out of my way to compliment others. It was like I had despised my mom so much that I vowed to never be like her. I couldn't understand how a woman would decide to keep a child just to make sure they were miserable. My mom did not have a good upbringing. She grew up in San Francisco, CA. They were extremely poor, and her stepfather beat her mom often. It was sad to hear her talk about it. I felt bad for my mom for the longest time, because I knew she was damaged, and angry

28

from her past trauma. She wasn't much of an emotional person, I remember her saying one time after she had quite a few glasses of wine say, "I'm mad at my mom for dying." It was evident that she was hurting, but I also despised the fact that she felt as if her mom did it on purpose. For a woman to grow up so poor, and have so little, she sure did portray a most selfish way of thinking. My mom was exceptionally angry when she drank. It wasn't even like she had to be drunk to get there, it was almost an easy countdown to see her become the ticking time bomb she was. It would be as quick as two sips into wine and she would get this look in her eye. I was constantly nervous around her when she was drinking because she would click into this gear where she wanted a fight and I was the target.

## Chapter Eleven

As Jed and my mom had continued their on again off again marriage, my mom continued to be despised anything I said and did. I was the punching bag. Between school, soccer, working, and trying to get some older guy to love me, I was stressed. I was at risk of almost being unable to graduate because my grades were slipping. I was so bad at soccer I decided not to play my senior year. I let it go, I was disappointed in myself. How did I go from being a star soccer player my entire life, to a girl who could barely control the ball? It made no sense to me at the time, but now I see my mindset and my goals were not in a healthy alignment.

One night I was getting ready to go somewhere with my girlfriends and my mom was in a mood. Clearly mad about Jed, but ready to hate me for it. She was furious and, in a rage, my friends were heading over and pick me up. She was screaming at me about something, and I was starting to get nervous knowing that she didn't care who witnessed it, she enjoyed seeing me worry about being embarrassed. It was almost like she would get another rise out of it seeing me coward down begging her not to yell so loudly because people could hear us. She would get even louder if I mentioned something like that. I hated scenes and hated how crazy she acted. I was sensitive, it wasn't one of those things where I just knew she was crazy and could go on about my day, it debilitated me at times. I have OCD, obsessive compulsive behavior. I've had it since I could remember. It wasn't a form of OCD where I was performing rituals and had to touch a doorknob a certain amount of times, it was more so this debilitating perfectionism that I struggled with. I internalized everything and hated the thought of "unfished business" or "unresolved issues." I would obsess and think and think to the point where I couldn't sleep. Which in turn, explains why I pulled my eyelashes out. It was self-mutilation, mixed with a sense of wanting to feel like I had the ability to make everything perfect. Nothing in my life was ever in my control, everything was taken from me including the roof over my head at one point. I lived in constant fear that if my mom wasn't pleased then she would boot me again.

As my friends told me they were about to pull up, and seeing my mom continue to scream at me, I was getting frustrated. She knew they were almost at our house and didn't care. Even if my friend's stayed in their car, I knew they could hear it from outside, and if my friends came to the door, it would be even more noticeable. I couldn't wait outside for them because my mom was not done screaming at me and if I dared walk away mid scream she would freak, and or follow me outside to cuss me out in front of the world. So, I had to sit there and take it. I finally said something snotty, which by now seventeen-year-old self clearly knew this would trigger her, but I felt as if I had nothing to lose, she wasn't calming down regardless and clearly enjoyed the fact that she was doing the one thing I hated most, making me nervous about a scene. "Are you on your period?" I said in a snippy, yet nervous tone. My mom went red. She screamed and before I knew it, she pulled down her pants and underwear to exposing her vagina, smacks her bare thighs and screams, "Does it look like I'm on my fucking period!" She ripped her pants down so fast I was shocked they didn't rip. It was at that moment that I feel as if I lost total respect for her. I was disgusted. Disgusted was the only word for it. I was a teenager and knew that I would never act like this. I would never ever show someone, let alone my kid my own vagina out of anger. I remember looking at her and saying, "What is wrong with you?" I didn't care how disrespectful my question was, I didn't respect her, and I genuinely wanted to know. I wanted her to feel stupid, embarrassed, and I wanted her to know that I am not going to act like this was normal. This was not normal. I know all families have their issues, they fight, they argue, etc. But what mom shows their kid their vagina? My question triggered her clearly, which was my goal. She screamed and said, "Fuck you, you fucking cunt." Just when I felt as if it couldn't get worse. She called me that. I had a foul mouth and cursed myself, but that word was the one word I never used or hoped to be called. And here I was called that, by my own mother.

I continued to focus on my social life, and Matt. I rarely spoke to anyone about how my mom really was. I hated the thought of people feeling sorry for me, and I was embarrassed. My mom was so hot and cold. She had this way of always being so giving to people who were struggling and needed help, but never enjoyed being in the company of people who were successful. It was odd for me; I am in full support of helping others, but my mom did it in a way where it wasn't so much "giving back," it was like she would be more giving to others and not me. Everything was conditional and held over my head, but she would help anyone else without question. It's not like she would donate or help feed the hungry. It was like her friends, or even sometimes my friends who needed help. My mom's friend would say, "I love your mom, she has her issues but if I needed something she would be there." For the longest time I agreed with this whole heartedly. Although she was fucked up to me, I loved how she has a big heart for others. But then I realized, she was only willing to help people who were faced with real drama. My mom was a fighter, she loved and enjoyed any chance to get in a fight. When she was growing up, she has been in multiple fist fights; she even beat someone up while she was pregnant with me. I had never been in a fist fight; I couldn't even imagine getting into an altercation with someone like that. If there was a fight, or someone needed to be scared, my mom would rise to the occasion. The friend that said my mom would "always be there" was a friend who was arrested one night during a domestic altercation. My mom enjoyed this sort of rush about being the "hero" but only if it meant giving her the chance to make someone fear her. If someone in our life had ultimate success, beauty, and goals, my mom did not want to be around them. I understand now, she was highly insecure, with an ego, and not a hero.

Chapter Twelve

Jed was off doing his own thing, traveling, and of course making my mom angry and spiteful about it. He was always going to Thailand, and Mexico for these long trips further distancing himself from my mom. I was a senior in high school and getting closer to being eighteen. Matt and I were still hanging out, he was a total loser, but I didn't know any better. He was getting evicted from his house and I told my mom he had nowhere to go. She let him move in with us, he had his own room, and it all just happened so fast. My mom and Jed were sharing custody of Caley and Tyler. Matt was paying rent and officially my boyfriend at this point. Jed found out about him living there and our relationship and quickly got the police involved. An

Officer came over to our house to inspect the living situation, my mom's reasoning for letting him live with us was because he was paying rent. Merely renting a room from us to help her out financially. When the officer came over, they interviewed myself and him, my stepdad wanted him arrested for statutory rape and this would also help him in court for getting full custody. Jed loved control; he loved power. He didn't even truly want Caley and Tyler full time, but he wanted to be a "winner." My mom also had this same mentality, she loved control. They were a terrible match, and still legally married. I remember running downstairs to Matt's room before the Officer came down and quickly grabbed a framed picture of me, from my senior photos that he had on his dresser. The officer scanned the room, and it looked legitimate. His own room, his own things, and no foul play to a stranger's eye.

Matt only lived with us for about a month before finding a studio to move into. I was almost eighteen, and my mom didn't even care for me to be around, so I stayed mostly with him. I was still in high school and practically living with my now twenty-seven-year-old boyfriend. I barely went to school; I showed up to the classes I was failing in hopes to get attendance credit at the very least because I was worried, I wasn't going to graduate. I was good at English, but terrible at Math. I cheated on tests all the time. I was able to just barely raise my grades up enough to finally graduate.

Graduation day was here. I was at my mom's house getting ready for my big day. Although I was always with Matt, I still had my room and belongings at my mom's. My mom got started a huge fight with me because now her and Jed her working on things yet again, and she had said that me moving Matt in was the reason she almost lost her kids. I was dumbfounded. How could she say that? She knew Matt and I were seeing each other, she let him move in, he had a damn picture of me in his room, I had a full-on stressful confession to her about his age! What was she saying? This lie my mom was running with was insane to me. It made zero sense. I almost wondered if she was trying to convince herself that she knew nothing about our relationship in hopes to make herself look better to Jed. As if this was all my fault that she almost lost custody and she would never condone such a relationship. She wanted to look like the golden mother, the perfect wife for Jed. She screamed at me, as I was trying to get my cap and gown together. Repeatedly shouting, "You lied to me about you two being together, you almost made me lose my fucking kids." I finally looked at her in disbelief and said, "That's not true mom! I literally cried to you one night about telling you the truth about Matt and you asked if he robbed a bank, if he killed someone, and all these crazy questions when I told you how old he was! I remember EVERYTHING about that night!" She refused to admit that conversation had ever happened. I was sick to my stomach, literally sick. I couldn't believe my own mother was lying, to me, to make me look like I was made this up. I had tears in my eyes as I grabbed my things and drove to high school for my graduation. My mom was going to be there to watch me graduate and I don't think she ever came.

I was standing with all my friends, and my entire graduating class on the football field, on such a beautiful sunny day when they finally announced, "Congratulations Class of 2007!" We all cheered and threw our caps high in the air. It was amazing, we felt free, we felt independent, we felt like life was just beginning. Everyone's family came walking out on to the field to hug and congratulate them. I circled around, looking and hoping to see my family. Everyone was hugging, holding flowers, balloons and taking pictures. But I had no one. No one was there. I wasn't going to invite Matt, it wasn't appropriate for him to be there, and with all the previous statutory accusations I didn't need my friend's family members seeing him either. I wanted my mom. I really wanted my mom. She was nowhere to be found. I was trying so hard to get out of there without making it obvious I had tears in my eyes. I felt a lump in my throat trying to fake a smile as if I had a purpose in the direction I was walking. I didn't, I wanted it to seem like I knew where my family was, but I didn't. I wanted to get to my fucking car and scream.

My mom had invited my Great Aunt and Uncle up from Oakland, CA for my graduation party. They were all back at my mom's house waiting for me. I drove straight there, trying to brush it off. Hoping there was some sort of fun to be had. All my friends had these huge graduation parties with their families. Some had a huge barbeque at their house, or they went to a nice dinner. For me, it was chips and dip and two of my family members along with Caley, Tyler, and Emma, our babysitter. It wasn't the food, or the location of my graduation party that bothered me, it was the energy. My mom had just pitched this bullshit alibi to me prior to my graduation, I was alone on that field, and I couldn't believe this was the story she was running with. I was also angry she was back with Jed; it was clear I was feeling even more alone because she had her husband back with their two kids they always wanted, and my mom was plotting this story against me. I hated graduation day.

## Chapter Thirteen

I was officially living with Matt now. I had little to no contact with my mom and was working at the restaurant still. I had no plans to go to college, nothing. I was going to be just like the rest of the twenty to thirty something year old losers who worked in a restaurant and lived paycheck to paycheck. It seemed cool when I was sixteen and seventeen, but I was poor, we were poor. My mom didn't help me out financially, that stopped when I was sixteen. Matt was always broke, and I was making a whole $6.75 an hour. I needed a change; I didn't even want to be in Tahoe anymore. Matt was a chef; he was an amazing cook actually and I knew he could take his talent elsewhere. Sandy, who I lived with when I was fed ex'd to Napa, CA was an Esthetician. She owned a Day Spa down there, and I loved it. I loved the spa like environment, I loved learning about skin, and facials. It was something about being able to completely relax someone and make them feel safe and at ease was enticing to me. I wanted to go to school to be an Esthetician.

I was sitting in the gross duplex that Matt and I had moved into, when I thought of this. I wanted to move back to Napa, but this time on my own terms. Sandy could teach me her ways and mentor me, and Matt could work in a restaurant down there. He was from Santa Rosa, CA which was close to Napa, so he had previous connections with people in the restaurant industry. Then I remembered, my dad lived in Napa. He moved to Colorado temporarily then moved back to Napa when I was twelve. I hadn't spoken to him since my mom put it in my head and accused him of molesting me. I'll never forget that voicemail he left me in utter disgust of my mom for saying such things. I remembered his phone number; I picked up the phone and called him. My stomach was in knots as the phone rang, what was I going to say? What if he hated me? He has a right to, I allowed my mom to convince me of something

I had no true memory about. Nothing in this world is lower and more evil than a pedophile, and my mom had no problem throwing that in my head about him. If she truly felt that way and believed that, then why didn't she have him arrested? Why didn't she pursue anything legally? Why did she let me fly to visit him when he lived in Colorado? It wasn't adding up as all this was flooding my brain further pushing me to validate why I should call him. The phone rang until I got his voicemail. It was the same voicemail I had remembered from years ago; it was nostalgic. "Dad." My voice cracked, "it's Candi, I just want to say I love you, and I'm sorry." I hung up. I didn't know what else I could say. I hoped he didn't want to call and talk to me about that specific allegation, I hoped he would call me, and we could just pick up where we left off. We actually had something in common, we both hated my mom. He called me back and it wasn't weird at all, we caught up briefly but didn't make any plans to see each other. I think it was almost as if we were scared of each other. Just with the allegations, it seemed like we both needed more time. But it was nice to break the ice and to feel like we were okay and didn't hate me.

My mom and I weren't really speaking, and I was ready to move away. I had talked to Matt about my ideas, and he was in full support of it. The only thing about moving was I couldn't bring JoJo with me. Not yet at least, if we were going to rent a place it wasn't one that I could take her to just yet. I had no credit and Matt had bad credit, and bad tenant history. He had been evicted numerous times from previous rentals. We were off to the great start. He had two dogs already that lived with us, and he would sneak them into rentals and keep them in his car when he had to go places. I couldn't do that to JoJo. No way, she was my world, and selfishly I wanted her with me everywhere I went, but I wasn't going to give her a pathetic living situation. JoJo had a good setup at my mom's, but it broke my heart the thought of leaving town without her. I promised her and myself I would be back for her.

In our duplex we didn't have a washer or dryer, but Matt had no problem walking into the vacant unit's garage next to us to see there was a perfectly working washer and dryer in there. We would sneak over and do our laundry. Matt would always get home late from working odd catering jobs and side gigs here and there and I was now working at a tanning salon and a breakfast restaurant. He always smelt like something unfamiliar. His saliva was different smelling and tasting, it wasn't like alcohol, this was different. I started to notice when he was home, he would always say he was going to go rotate laundry. He'd mosey his way over there, then come back twenty minutes later, sit with me and then go rotate again. I started to catch on with how odd this was seeing as there really weren't any more clothes left to wash. I waited a bit after he said he was going to rotate the laundry again, then I quietly walked over to the vacant unit's garage. We had only gone in the garage never inside the actual empty duplex itself. I opened the door slowly and saw the washer and dryer, but no sign of Matt. I had an eerie feeling, I started to slowly make my way towards the door that enters the duplex. It was open, I saw Matt standing in the empty kitchen facing the counter. He saw me and I froze, "What are you doing?" I yelled, he bolted towards me blocking my view of what was in the kitchen. He kept saying "Nothing! Nothing!" as he was holding a rolled up hundred-dollar bill in his hand. I didn't know what that meant. I was too scared to push through to see what it was in the kitchen. Not because I feared him, but because I was scared of entering someone's actual house. The garage was enough for me, it felt like I was violating someone entirely had I walked into the house. I ran back into our duplex shaking and confused. "What was that? Why was he holding a rolled up hundred-dollar bill?" I thought to myself. I had no clue what this meant, but my gut was telling me something was off.

Matt came back inside and I of course questioned him. "What was that? What were you doing over there? Are you drinking?" his face looked relieved almost, "Yes, Candi. I have a drinking problem." My innocent brain and lack of street smarts clearly fed him an easy alibi. He managed to run with a "drinking problem" story. I was so upset thinking my boyfriend was an alcoholic and how we were going to get through this. He quickly convinced me that it was the people he was surrounded by like his coworkers that were the bad influence. And that us moving to Napa was going to make things better for him and us. So, we made the move.

We rented house in Vacaville, CA. About twenty minutes from Napa, with his terrible credit and poor rental history and my nothing, we rented a place under his name by some sketchy Indian guy who didn't even live in the area. It was the only place that would accept us, so it was oddly simple getting the keys, probably because we were the only tenants who ever inquired about the place. This house was in the ghetto, moving boxes in from my 4-runner was even scary, if you took ten steps, someone was already looking inside your car. As I set a few boxes down in this cold, uninviting house, I opened an odd-looking container I found in Matt's things, it was a glass pipe. I was different looking, I've seen a weed pipe before, but this was clear and different, it didn't smell like burnt weed at all, but I just assumed it was. I wasn't a fan of weed and Matt knew I wouldn't be with him if he smoked, he didn't smoke weed so I assumed it was from back in his younger days. All of a sudden, a woman walked right into the house. I quickly turned around just frozen and speechless. She wasn't wearing shoes and had crazy curly black hair, her head was twitching in every different direction. "Hey!" she squeaked out. "Hi….?" I stammered. "This used to be a crack house. Yep!" And murmured a few more things and walked out. My stomach felt sick, what were we getting ourselves into? I didn't feel safe at all. Not to mention, the backyard had a man living in it. Yep, a man in a broken-down RV, in our backyard. The landlord did not disclose this to us, and we didn't ask him about it because we were the type of tenants that didn't reveal the fact that we also had Matt's two dogs living with us. Matt was a professional shitty tenant, and now I was too.

Matt was working at a pizza shack; he was the manager there. I had officially enrolled into Beauty College. I was busy with school and didn't want to live with Matt in that old crack house anymore because I didn't feel safe alone there and he worked late. I asked to live with Sandy again in Napa. I commuted from her house to school every day and was doing well. I got a job at a restaurant in Napa as a busser. I'd go to school full time, worked late and kept my focus. My 4-runner was giving me problems and I needed a reliable car because my commute to school was an hour there and an hour back. Sandy's husband was kind enough to work on my car for me, but I needed a new car and fast.

I called my great Aunt Mary, who lived in Oakland, Ca. She didn't have any kids herself. She was the one who came to my ever so uplifting graduation party. She had money, she didn't have any children herself, a somewhat crotchety woman, set in her ways but always in support of anyone furthering their education. I called her and asked her if she would loan me the money to buy a new car. I told her I was just looking for a used car under $9,000. She was older, and didn't always have the best advice, and said "Well I think it would be better if we lent you the money for a new car, it's more reliable." My eyes lit up. A new car? I had the ability to get a new car? I couldn't contain myself; I was so excited. Not knowing how stupid this was considering I was barely making any money and I set up a plan with her to make monthly payments. But I was fully confident that I could do this, because my plan was to be a successful esthetician and possibly own a day spa one day like Sandy.

My great aunt and uncle met me at a dealership, and I picked out a new Toyota Corolla. I was so excited and so grateful. I loved my new car. I told my mom about it as well, even though we barely spoke, I would still check in from time to time. My plan was to sell my 4-runner so I could finally have some money, I was struggling. I could barely afford gas. I would overdraw my account to put gas in. I would only get about $8 in tips as a busser, and sometimes my tips would get stolen from the other co-workers. The servers would leave them in an envelope and leave them in a bowl with our name on it, and mine would go missing often. Me being young and in fear of confrontation, I never asked the owner to have a better system or even pay me for my rightful payouts. I just allowed things to happen because I hated potential confrontation.

Chapter Thirteen

I was officially in my last quarter of esthetician school and excelling. I wasn't really in contact with Matt much, I sort of drifted away after moving in with Sandy and focusing on school. He had transferred to a new location with the pizza shack and moved to Napa as well and living in a townhouse there. I didn't really care much, because I was focused on school and I always met this guy at my gym, Gio. Gio was buff, really buff and had big blue eyes and beautiful olive skin. He was friends with a mutual friend of mine, so I was introduced to him. He had a girlfriend though, she was pretty, but I had heard their relationship was toxic and he was a major flirt. I backed off after hearing he had a girlfriend, but when I did it was like he flirted more. I enjoyed the chase, but it was never going to be more than that unless he was willing to be single.

I was constantly living under paycheck to paycheck, struggling to get by. I was lucky enough to live with Sandy for free, but I still had bills. I had my phone, car insurance, a commute, bridge toll, and now an official car payment. My 4-runner was for sale. I was selling it for $2,500. It was in great shape but had 234k miles on it. This was my only chance to have any sort of help financially.

My mom called me and said she wanted to come down and see me. I was shocked, and so excited. I couldn't believe she actually wanted to come see me. She said she was going to drive down with Emma, our babysitter growing up but practically our adopted cousin. My mom was still with Jed of course which was another reason why I was shocked she was going to make the over three-hour drive to come see me, but I was excited. She said she would come see me at my school, and even get a facial from me, and book a hair appointment with one of the students at my school. I was so close with all my classmates; I couldn't wait for her to meet my new friends. I even made sure I booked my mom with my favorite future cosmetologist there. She had done my hair quite a few times, and I made sure my mom was booked with her.

When my mom and Emma got there, I gave them a tour, they met all my friends and professors, and I hooked my mom up with all the free services she could get. Her hair looked amazing, and it was so nice to see her and Emma. I asked my mom if she was going to stay the night with me at Sandy's house. My mom took me by surprise when she said, "No, Emma and I are driving back tonight. We came down to pick up the 4-runner." My jaw dropped. I felt as if all the blood rushed from my face, and I could melt to the floor. "What?" I asked, with barely any energy to form a word. "Yes, were going to pick up the 4-runner, and Emma will drive it back. Jax needs a car." I was sick, literally sick to my stomach. How could I be so stupid? To actually think she came down here to see me, to see how well I was doing. She had a plan all along. She never called to talk to me, to check on me, to see if I was doing okay, and here she was, to use me. The 4-runner was mine; I had the title to it, it was in my name and legally mine. I couldn't believe she thought I was that stupid. "Mom, I need to sell it. I need that money." My mom snaps and said, "Jax needs a car." I was furious at this point. Why the fuck would I give up my one and only chance to get my bank account out of constant overdraft fees and be able to actually fill up my tank without praying my card doesn't get declined to help Jed! Jed! Jed's son Jax. Why would I do anything to help that man out. Jax wasn't my son, nor was he my brother as he kindly reminded me of every day growing up together. Why the fuck would I do that? I was nervous, I couldn't even believe I was about to stand up to her, but I stayed firm. "No." I said. "Jed can buy it from me." My mom was livid. She could barely see straight. She called me about every four-letter word in the book. And then proceeded to try and "guilt trip" me with the story of "you almost got my kids taken away by saying you weren't in a relationship with a twenty-six-year-old you fucking bitch." There it was, her famous lie. I knew she was sick in the head. She loved to resort to something so low in attempt to get her way. She threw these low blows my entire life and on top of that the lie that I knew deep down she was trying to tell herself was true. Fuck her, is all I could think. She and Emma drove back up to Tahoe, and we had no further contact.

I felt so low, betrayed, and used. So incredibly used. How dare she? How dare Jed to think I would help him out like that? Even Sandy, her own friend thought it was messed up. She knew how broke I was, and how hard I've been struggling. How could my mom play me like that? How ingenuine my own mother was. I was hurt. I needed a security blanket; I needed a distraction, I needed to feel love. I called Matt.

## Chapter Fourteen

Matt and I rekindled, and we were doing well. I was now a licensed esthetician. I was so proud of myself for accomplishing this on my own and was ready to work at a day spa. Matt's sister Sarah and I were close, she lived in Los Angeles. We talked almost every day on the phone. She had an extremely wealthy fiancé and a fun social life. Sarah was beautiful, she had this dirty blonde hair, and gorgeous complexion, her eyes were hazel, and she was so thin. It was an unhealthy thin, but for LA, that was the norm. Matt and I flew to LA for her wedding, and it was amazing. I loved the fast city life. I loved meeting Sarah and her fiancés friends and seeing how they lived. I wasn't even twenty-one yet, but I sure acted like it, and LA sure treated me like it.

One day during our trip, Sarah recommended that Matt and I should move down there. They had all these friends and connections in the restaurant industry which was perfect for Matt. And I was a licensed Esthetician so I could go easily apply to one of the many day spas they had. LA was full of people with money, which is the industry Matt and I both needed to work for. We were at one of Matt's uncles houses. They had a beautiful home in Glendale, Ca. One thing I loved, is every single boyfriend I've ever had, has always had the best families. Their dynamic was so healthy and fun loving. I found it fascinating everyone could easily have dinner and cocktails and not a single fight would break out. I wasn't used to that, people just really enjoying each other's company. We were all ready to go in the hot tub with everyone after dinner. I was changing into my bathing suit in the bathroom. Then I heard Sarah and Matt's mom Donna laughing together down the hall. They were cracking up about something. Just the two of them, literally laughing so hard. It was the sweetest thing in the world to witness, but it made me sad. I leaned against the bathroom door and just started crying. I couldn't help but be so jealous of Sarah and her relationship with her mom. Their entire family loved, and laughed, and smiled. Sure, they had their moments, but it wasn't where anyone would call each other the "C" word. I looked in the mirror and tried to dry my tears. I wasn't good at making it obvious I wasn't crying because my eyes would get so red and swollen. I took a deep breath and convinced myself to snap out of it. I walked out of the bathroom and got in the hot tub with everyone and enjoyed the rest of the night.

Matt and I decided we were going to move to LA. It was an exciting change for us, and it seemed full of opportunities. I had applied at a fancy Day Spa in West Hollywood. I had to go back down there for an interview and then again for a hands-on interview. They were extremely impressed by me which was surprising because I was fresh out of school. There were about nine other applicants, all who had experience and I beat them out of the job. I was so excited. We had to move down there rather quickly because I accepted the job offer and I needed to start by a certain date.

Here we were again, faced with a new application to fill out for a rental. With Matt's terrible credit, and rental history. Let's add breaking leases to his list of credentials. We were rejected almost everywhere we applied to. Matt came home one day so excited and said he found us a place. He said it was a cute little apartment and they were even okay with dogs. He said the landlord lived out of the country helping the less fortunate but was willing to send us the keys today if we wired the money. Matt was ready to make it happen. "Hold on." I said, "this seems sketchy Matt, almost too good to be true." Matt didn't like my negativity, but I asked if he could show me the ad for the place. I clicked into gear, I started to scan the ad and noticed the ad continuously said, "flat for rent" not "apartment." That verbiage alone didn't line up with anyone from the states. Sure, people from out of the country could absolutely sell or rent properties, but they at least know the verbiage America uses. That was my first clue, then the "landlord" stated he was helping the less fortunate in Nigeria. "What a cliché thing to say" I thought to myself. I looked at his "website" of his volunteer work and noticed multiple spelling errors on the site. The entire thing was a scam, and my much older than me boyfriend was ready to wire him the little money we had within two seconds had I not stepped in.

Then we landed on a studio apartment that accepted our application. We didn't even look at the apartment prior to moving in because we couldn't afford to keep flying or driving back and forth to LA. This apartment was in Los Feliz. It was titled "Little Armenia." We signed papers and made the move. This apartment was on the third floor of this old, dark, dingy building. The elevators were broken, and even if they were working, I wouldn't dare risk it. The building was falling apart. It offered street parking only and no air conditioning. But I was excited to live there. Our apartment was cooking with heat on the top floor when LA would hit a hundred degrees. I would often take the dogs to the dog park and sleep under a tree it was so hot. The building was run by a slumlord. There were multiple articles about her online and we were starting to experience it ourselves. We knew we weren't living in a five-star high rise, but between the cockroach infestation and all the creeps that would walk in and sleep in the halls of our building, it was bad.

Matt didn't have any luck finding a job at a restaurant yet, so the building manager hired him to do maintenance work around the building. The owner was going to pay him to fix up damaged units so they could be ready to rent to the next tenant. The building managers were this cute couple from South America. They were such kind people, and they too hated how the owner handled the place.

I was making minimum wage at the day spa because it was required for all us estheticians to go to an eight-week training course in Studio City before officially performing services on clients at our respective locations. This training was intense, eight hours a day, five days a week in a studio warehouse, and we had to test out. If you didn't pass you couldn't work for them. It was like Esthetician boot camp. Seeing as I wasn't making much money to cover any of the bills, and we had one car, my corolla, we were limited on access to other jobs for Matt. Matt didn't have a license, and owed hundreds of dollars to the DMV, so this didn't help either. The money I got from selling my 4-runner prior to moving to LA went quick. I had to pay Sandy's husband back for the car parts he bought to fix the 4-runner up, a few car payments later, and paying about eight hundred dollars just to get my back account back up to zero dollars. The money was gone. We were broke, we would get food at the dollar store and purposely get easy-mac because easy-mac didn't require milk just water, we couldn't afford much.

About five weeks had gone by and Matt was never paid for his work he was doing for the apartment building. The owner kept telling him that the check was on the way, but it never was. We were struggling, and it was sad. One day during our day spa training, one of the girl's said that it was someone in our training's course's birthday the next day and asked if we all wanted to pitch in five dollars to get her something. We were all so close by then, it felt like a sorority. Everyone said they would pitch in and then when it became my turn I, for the first time broke down in front of people. I never liked showing vulnerability, especially since I was always known as the positive, uplifting, entertainer of the group. My face fell to my hands, and I just cried out, "I'm sorry... I'm just so broke." I couldn't believe I had said that out loud. It was so embarrassing. My colleagues were all so understanding and supportive. To this day I am grateful for how they treated me during that moment.

I got home that day from a long day of training to a letter taped on my apartment door. I took it off and saw "Three Days to Pay Rent or Quit." I couldn't believe it, my name was officially on this lease, and I was going to have an eviction on my record, I was furious. Matt walked in and I was enraged. Not at him, at the audacity the landlord has! She hadn't paid Matt for his labor at all and has the nerve to expect rent. The least she could have done was trade work for rent. I was angry, I took a red sharpie and wrote "FUCK YOU" on the notice and marched downstairs to the building manager's office. It was the cute South African couples' office/ home as well. I didn't write this as a note to them, because I knew they were doing this on behalf of Monica, the slumlord. So I slid it right under their door so they could relay the message. They knew how she was and how many people Monica has taken advantage of, they were quite proud of me.

The building managers managed to secretly tell me that Monica was coming to the property that following day. They hated her just as much, as she took advantage of them too. They were a hard-working older couple with health problems, and she was burning them to the ground, and they were getting threatened by the tenants daily. This was the moment I was waiting for. To give her a piece of my mind. I would have called her, but no one had her number. Everything was via e-mail. I waited until the time I knew she was arriving, I walked down the stairs from my cockroach infested apartment and saw her at the end of the hall, I stormed straight up to her and said, "Look at you, with your fucking Jimmy Choo shoes as you scam people out of money, you fucking slimy piece of shit. Go ahead try and evict me, this entire building isn't up to code, everything here is highly illegal, including the prostitutes that take clients here. Try me bitch!" I don't know what came over me, but it came out perfect. She was terrified, so terrified that she called the cops on me. And of course, they didn't do a thing to me, the person doing something illegal here was her.

We stayed in that apartment a little longer, cockroaches ran across my face almost nightly as I slept. The street parking was almost impossible. If I ever parked in a spot that was close to the building, someone would deflate my tires. This happened about twice a week. It was risk to park close or park two miles away in an unsafe area and walk by myself to and from my apartment. Nothing good came from this living situation. Matt finally got a job at Guitar Center. He had a hobby of DJing. He had DJ equipment and has worked a few events in the past. He was able to make commission at Guitar Center which helped us financially. I was officially working as an Esthetician at the Day Spa in West Hollywood and had a second job working at Hollywood Tans. We were finally able to grocery shop, and sometimes go out to dinner here and there. We broke our lease and moved into a better apartment in Hollywood. I wasn't worried for one second about breaking our lease seeing as the landlord was a known slumlord and had multiple court cases against her, in addition to our building not being up to code in any way shape or form. Our new place wasn't in the greatest area, but it had underground parking and the building was much nicer. You also needed a key to enter the building. I was so happy to be in a building where this time the only crack heads that roamed the halls were the ones that lived there. What a sense of appreciation.

After a few months working at the Day Spa, the recession hit. There were eleven Estheticians, and the day spa was laying off six of us. I was shocked to find out I wasn't one of them. The other's had so much more experience and had been there for longer, but I had almost record-breaking sales and wonderful reviews from my clients.

We would make commission on the products we sold, and I studied how they wanted us to push the products on our clients after each service. This wasn't effective to me, I found that I would show my client all the products I used on their skin, but if I had to choose my favorite two for them, I'd slide them forward. Therefore, it didn't come across as "here buy all twelve of these products now!" It was more of an honest recommendation in a conservative way, and quite effective.

At the tanning salon, I loved my coworkers. It was such a fun job, and it blew my mind how we were told to give any and all "A list" celebrities free memberships and lotions. Sure, I could see how it would be great for business and advertising, but I was blown away by how they were the only people in the world who could even afford anything, and they get free stuff. It was comical, but of course I complied. We had a team meeting one day, and seeing as I was the new girl, I knew my sales and commission wasn't going to be as great as everyone else. As the manager started talking during the meeting, he said, "Candi is by far our biggest MVP here." My jaw dropped, I almost got shy for the first time in my life. How could that be? My sales weren't nearly as good as the other girls, I also hated sounded like a car salesman vulture. I was good at the day spa because the approach was different, but selling tanning lotion didn't seem as genuine to me. Scott, my manager was complimenting my customer service, and how many kind words he has received about me. I almost wanted him to stop complimenting me because I could see one of the other girls who had been working there the longest get mad. She was jealous yes, but I didn't want her to be. I would often get worried if someone complimented me in front of other people because I always worried it would make others feel less than me. I literally start to panic when this happens. I enjoy being recognized for my hard work, but not in front of my peers. It has always been something that bothered me, and it's usually because I was used to girls being mean to me afterwards. I feel like it's because I was always the black sheep of my family and I knew what it was like to be the least favorite, so I hated the thought of anyone else having to experience that, even on a career level.

## Chapter Fifteen

Sarah and her husband Roger had a seemingly beautiful life. He came from so much money and Sarah was so madly in love with him and was going to have it all. I blew my mind how she was so attracted to him. He was a grungy looking man with dark, thin, streamy hair. He had a belly and dark circles under his eyes. He told everyone he was a movie producer, but that was more of a typical LA motto. Everyone in LA called themselves actress, models, or producers, yet they weren't, not yet at least. Roger had money because his mommy and daddy had money. He was an only child and his parents lived in Bel Air, one of nicest, most expensive parts of LA.

Roger's parents were kind enough to have Matt and I over for dinner with Sarah and Roger from time to time. Their house was stunning. Everything was so detailed, such beautiful art pieces, a pool, a maid, custom themes in every bedroom. It was incredible just to say I had been inside a house in Bel Air let alone dine in one. Roger's parents were very kind. Yes, they spoiled the hell out of their adult baby Roger, but they were very welcoming to Matt and myself, I loved how they included us.

Matt still wasn't having any luck finding a restaurant job, but guitar center seemed to be working well for him. We had a good relationship; it really wasn't that unhealthy. We drank a lot though. I loved wine with dinner, and he loved anything he could get his hands on. One night Matt and I went out with some of his friends from the Guitar Center, I wasn't even twenty-one yet, but I got into every bar no problem. Matt and I walked back to our apartment and I was very drunk and spinning badly. We had our usual drunk sex and I passed out naked. I was woken up a short while later to a weird flash before my eyes, I thought I was dreaming so I didn't care to open my eyes much and just passed back out.

The next morning, I woke up and went to work at the Day Spa. I would walk two miles to work. I had a car but the parking in West Hollywood was ridiculous. Every day there was a different rule about when and where you could park. I managed to get three parking tickets in one day. That scared me straight, I chose to walk the two miles to and from work down Hollywood Blvd. I lived closer to the tanning salon so that was an easier commute on foot. But I enjoyed walking, I was so used to the city life and the culture, and I would take the time to call my friends and catch up with them during my walks. I also lost a lot of weight.

By the time I got back to my apartment after my shift, Matt was still working. He wasn't going to be home until a few hours later. I looked over and saw his digital camera on the dresser. Something told me to look through it. I turned it on and started scrolling through the recent photos. These were photos of me, naked. Not only naked, but practically unconscious. He took these without me even knowing, and that's what the flash was that slightly woke me up the night before. The photos looked sickening. I felt violated because these weren't like tasteful nudes that a boyfriend would want of his girlfriend, these were of me completely helpless looking.

I put the camera down and froze for a bit. I didn't know what to say or how to react. Should I feel violated or flattered? I kept thinking how it was odd he would want photos of me like that, I would have been willing to take sexy pictures for him for his eyes only had he asked. But this seemed different. I kept convincing myself that I should just take it as a compliment and say nothing.

It was Christmas time and Sarah and Roger invited us to his parents for Christmas dinner. Matt's mom was also going to be there. I was so excited to go over there again, we would both dress nice and their butler would great us with fancy cocktails and we would all gather in this one fancy room. It was like what I would picture a "study" to look like for rich people. It was an elegant room for entertainment full of beautiful sculptures and books and we would just sit, and chat and I would stare at Roger's mom's jewelry she was wearing. She had the biggest diamonds in the world just bedazzled all over her. This was normal life to her; her rings were just things she'd throw on. I couldn't believe some people lived this way. Meanwhile my bank account was sitting at $2.65.

Sarah was handed a gift by Roger's mom, and so was I. My face lit up; I wasn't expecting a gift at all. I couldn't believe how kind she was to include me; she didn't have to do that. I opened my gift, and it was a brand-new Coach purse! The purse had to have been about $500. My face looked like it had seen a ghost. I had tears in my eyes, and I thanked her a million times over and over. I couldn't believe I got a brand-new coach purse. I loved it, I never wanted to leave this place. We all sat down for dinner and Roger's mom made a beautiful toast, she thanked all of us for being there and thanked Matt's mom for sharing her beautiful daughter with them. It was a beautiful, heartfelt speech that killed me. I was smiling big, almost forcefully because if I allowed my face to move at all, tears would roll down at any second. I was sad I didn't have a mom like theirs. Yes, they included me and made me feel like family, but it still broke my heart my mom wasn't a proud mom of me. Tears flowed down my cheeks at the dinner table, and I was humiliated. It seemed more awkward if I excused myself to go to the restroom because I knew if I got a moment alone, I would just cry harder. I didn't want any attention for it either. It was better for me to fight it. It was Christmas and my mom hadn't even called me. This day marked almost exactly one year since her and I spoke.

Chapter Sixteen

Same old thing, different day with us living in LA. Matt and I, with our mediocre jobs and not advancing or saving money at all. I was getting sick of it, there would be no way we could ever do better than we were. He was in debt beyond belief, no car, no license, no goals.
I decided to leave town for a weekend and go to Napa. I took the long six hour drive I vented to my friends on the phone about how I was getting over my relationship with Matt. I just wasn't into it anymore and I wanted a change. When I got to Napa and met up with some friends who were at a party. Gio was there, big buff Gio. He and I flirted the whole night, and I was like this spark went off in me. I was instantly over Matt. I didn't even care to call Matt that whole weekend.

As I drove home back to LA, I listened to all sorts of sappy love songs and fantasized about Gio. I wanted to move back to Napa and work at a spa there. I could live with Sandy and then eventually get my own place, and I wanted to go to school to become a Medical Assistant. I loved the medical field and wanted to learn more about it. I heard there was a good Medical Assisting program at the college in Napa and that's what my heart was set on.

I started to think about my relationship with Matt and really try to understand what was wrong with it. He made me feel beautiful and didn't cheat on me, but he had some issues that didn't sit right with me. He was baggage for me, his teeth were randomly cracking, and I was weirded out by the photos he took of me. I was starting to realize his teeth were cracking because of past or maybe even present drug use. I started making calls to get my ducks in a row, I called Sandy to tell her about my plan and she said that her father-in-law in Napa has a room at his house and they would let me live there with him and help look after him. He was old and lived alone. He was a sharp man but getting older for sure. That was a perfect plan. Gio and I were texting nonstop, and I was telling him about my plan which made him excited too. I kept picturing my new life and was enjoying the daydreaming about it all day long.

By the time I got back home to LA I had told Matt that I wanted to go back to school and was considering moving to Napa to pursue that. He was supportive but not excited obviously. I had a few weeks before I could make any decisions anyways. I needed to give both my jobs proper notice and figure out school in Napa as well. So, I had some time before actually saying goodbye. But yes, I was with my boyfriend and texting Gio all day long.

After a while I had heard that my mom and Jed were splitting up. Apparently, she caught him cheating with a woman in El Dorado Hills, Ca. He was clearly living a double life. My mom was devasted, and a close source had told me all about it. I didn't care to call; she has gone comfortably a full year without speaking to me and holiday after holiday went by bringing myself to tears each time. Screw her I thought, I hope she's happy with her choices.

Moving to Napa didn't go as quick as I planned. Sandy still had to talk to her father-in-law and get the room ready, and I hadn't given notice to my jobs yet. A couple months had gone by, but I still stuck to my plan of moving there, it was just slightly delayed. I just continued to work, and text Gio daily.

My stepsister Jenny called me, she said that her and her friends had been going up to Tahoe to party and they would stay with my mom. Jed was very strict and wouldn't condone a bunch of kids in their early twenties coming in and out of the house after being at the bars all night. Jenny said my mom was partying with them. She made it seem like it was fun and that she was keeping my mom out of depression due to her heartbreak from Jed.  Although my mom and Jed weren't together anymore, Jenny was still considered my sister, and my mom was still considered her stepmom. We grew up together, that doesn't just disappear after a divorce. I had mixed emotions about my mom partying with people around my age, but then I felt like maybe this was a good thing, so she wasn't crying every night. I was hoping this was just possibly a phase.

A few days later, I received a text… from my mom. "Candi, I miss you, an Angel came to visit me last night and has shown me love." I read that and started crying. I couldn't believe she reached out, and she was even talking about Angels? She has never been the type to talk about Angels or God ever. I had this warm feeling come over me and I was so incredibly happy. I wrote her back and I told her I was planning on moving back to Napa to go to school to be a Medical Assistant. She had said she would come down and help me move. I was so touched that she even wanted to help me.

It wasn't until a couple days later when I was talking to Jenny on the phone to tell her my mom and I reconnected and the beautiful text she sent me when Jenny said, "Candi, the Angel she is referring to is my friend Ian." "What?" I said, my stomach already in knots but hoping she was going to reassure me of something completely different. "Yeah, she slept with my friend Ian." "What the fuck?" I was disgusted. She was already smitten… over a twenty-three-year-old? Nope, this is not normal. Jenny glazed over the situation letting me know they weren't dating, but he just helped her come out of her shell a bit and boosted her confidence. I guess I felt like that could have been innocuous. I was a little uneasy about it all, but I didn't let it overwhelm me considering I was so excited and happy to have my mom back.

## Chapter Seventeen

A few weeks rolled by of consistent chatting with my mom again and getting excited about my plans. Sandy said the extra bedroom in her father-in-law's house was ready, so I was then ready to give proper notice at work. I decided to take a quick trip up to Tahoe to see my mom, and Jenny. I was only twenty years old but coming home and partying with my mom and stepsister seemed fun. I was extremely excited to see my dog JoJo. As I got there, she didn't leave my side. It was like no time had passed, she knew I was hers and she was mine. My plan was once I got settled in Napa, I would get a place of my own and bring her with me. But living in an elderly man's home for free was something I shouldn't press my luck on. My stepsister Jenny told me that my mom and her were hanging out with these guys that moved in across the street. It was three guys, Taylor, Scott, and Jake. They were closer to mine and Jenny's age than my mom's. My mom and Jed were sharing custody of Caley and Tyler, so they were back and forth.

One night I was having wine with my stepsister, mom, and a few friends when in walks in the three that lived across the street. "These are the guys they're hanging out with?" I thought to myself.

They seemed incredibly comfortable walking through the front door. My mom apparently had been sleeping with Jake. He had a chipped front tooth, and dirty fingers. This made complete sense because for work he was a "handy man." Which is typical for a guy like him with no resume, or drive. He apparently had a son, who was currently in juvenile hall. "What the hell is my mom doing?" I thought to myself. I continued to sip my wine just trying to go along with this new scene inside the house I helped build with my stepdad. Jake made his way over to me as I stood by our gas fireplace with my dog. He was extremely flirty, and before I knew it, he grabbed my butt. I instantly made a scene in a sarcastic way. I acted like it was funny but also making it clear to keep his hands off me. I purposely did this so my mom would notice, so she would realize these guys are garbage and this guy she was sleeping with would instantly hook up with me if he could. She laughed it off too and said "Jake, get your hands off my daughter you sicko." Desperately laughing with every word. "What, she's hot?" He slurred. He was a drunk, a sloppy drunk. He could hardly form a sentence, and just continued to drink beer like it was water. My mom and everyone else started taking shots of Whiskey. I couldn't believe this was going on. I was having fun yes, but still this just seemed inappropriate. If Jed knew this was going on, he would freak out.

It was getting late, I went to bed downstairs, JoJo came with me of course. Jenny ended up going out with some of her friends and Scott tagged along too. They had hooked up a few times, but Jenny was funny about it, she never took him seriously and she knew he was just Mr. Right now, not Mr. Right. Jenny wasn't the type to fall in love easily, or at all. I loved how she didn't take life too seriously. She always controlled her emotions and was incredibly intelligent. She didn't even have to try to be smart, she just was. I had to work for it when it came to academics, Jenny could just click into gear without having to study. She was quite emotionally unavailable to any man. When we were younger her mom made her and Jax move all the time. They were at a new school almost every year when we were growing up. I think she just became accustomed to never getting too comfortable.

The house was quiet, everyone had left. Including my mom. She went to the bars with Jake at this bar down the street from our house. When I woke up, she wasn't home. I felt uncomfortable as she came walking inside the house with her hair a complete mess. She stayed across the street at Jake's house. I felt like such a guest in the house I was trying to wrap my brain around this new household she was running.

I had to head back to LA, to start packing. Once I got back to the apartment I was just completely checked out. I was over LA, I was over Matt, and completely infatuated with Gio. We talked nonstop, but my friends in Napa constantly warned me about him. He was a bad boy and a total player, and I was attracted to that. For some reason I was so mesmerized by him. He was so different than Matt, and loved the gym, which I did too. He seemed to be more my style.

About a week later I was almost all packed. I was on the phone with Jenny, when she told me that she was no longer going up to my mom's to party anymore. She said it was getting out of hand and that her dad Jed was pissed. He had gotten wind of all the things my mom was doing and was threatening to take full custody. There were multiple witnesses about her behavior at the bars, as this was becoming a regular thing. Worst of all, she was having Jake over on the days she had Caley and Tyler. Since Caley and Tyler were only about twelve and thirteen, this strange man in their house bothered them, rightfully so. Tyler and Caley were both so upset one night Tyler walked upstairs and barged into our mom's room. They walked in on her having sex with Jake. Caley called her dad in tears and asked him to come get them. My mom, freaked out on them. She was furious my brother and sister made such a big deal about this. As if she was the victim. Jed was ready to take action legally.

I think my mom was more upset about potentially losing Jake more than Caley and Tyler. Jake was younger, a big partier, and still wanted the single life. My mom was a security blanket for him. He would call her while she was at work at 3:00pm to ask her to come pay his bar tab because he couldn't afford it. She happily did it, she loved doing it, she loved any excuse to see him and to feel needed by him. She ended up paying for his juvenile delinquent son's attorney's fees as well. She was extra giving with her money because she knew deep down that was the only thing that could keep him coming back for more. He would still go out, which was easy for him to get away with the things he wanted to do on the nights my mom was stuck having to be a mom for Caley and Tyler. She was angry because since Tyler walked in on her and they got their dad involved, she knew this could compromise her life she wanted with Jake. She knew she could no longer throw the parties she was throwing for Jake and his friends because of this, so this triggered her insecurities of not being able to keep tabs on Jake.

She was changing as a person, completely losing herself. She was getting more tattoos, and even got a dermal piercing. She was drinking more to match his lifestyle and gaining weight. Jake enjoyed rock crawling with his friends, which was basically just another drinking hobby where you bring beer and drive beat up trucks up rocks all day. My mom went with him once on a rock crawling camping trip and she wanted to be in their click so badly, she bought a truck and turned it into a rock crawler. She couldn't get enough of him, and she was disposable to him.

Jake started to go out and party more and it was driving my mom crazy. All she did was blame Jed for preventing her from having fun. She started to get spiteful and got drunk one night because she had heard Jake was hanging out with someone else. She ended up going across the street and sleeping with Scott. His roommate, the guy who also slept with Jenny multiple times. Jenny was also aware of this encounter; she didn't care about Scott, but she was certainly shocked my mom would go that low. My mom was acting out in attempt to get him jealous. I became good friends with Taylor, he was one of the three roommates. He was closer to my age, and I thought he had the best sense of humor. He was this short, stubby looking guy, not attractive but definitely the life of the party. He and I would text from time to time as friends only. I was embarrassed that it was my mom that always at their house bouncing from room to room. He knew she was crazy, and he also knew that Jake didn't have pure intentions with my mom. He tried to stay loyal as a friend to Jake, and not tell my mom all that he was doing, but my mom was purposely hanging out with Scott and Taylor trying to get as close as possible to Jake. It was like no one else existed in this world, just Jake.

## Chapter Eighteen

It was officially moving day for me. I was sad for Matt; he was so supportive of my dreams and goals which almost made it harder to leave. We had a good relationship, but I was so young, and fell completely out of love. I would often have flashbacks of finding him in that abandoned duplex, finding that glass pipe, and those nude photos of me while I was sleeping. I felt like he had his secrets but was good at keeping them. I knew he would be okay because his sister and her husband were there for him. He had such a good family; I didn't feel like I was leaving him stranded. He deserved to be with someone amazing, I wasn't that girl for him.

My mom drove to Napa and left her car at Sandy's so she could drive back to Tahoe from there, she flew down to LA and helped me load my car up. I didn't have much to move considering I was so young and broke I never had an opportunity to furnish any place I lived in. Matt had his furniture, and I had my clothes. We loaded up my Toyota Corolla and headed up to Napa. The whole time my mom was talking as if she was in her twenties. She was using all this slang that I didn't even use but Jake and his roommates did. She was so different, and still angry with Jed, any chance she got to talk about him about how she hates him and how he's trying to ruin her life she did. In all honesty, I didn't disagree with him. She was acting crazy, drinking a lot, getting in bar fights, and having parties at her house. I would refrain from saying that of course.

As we got to Napa, we stopped at Sandy's house before going over to her father in laws and getting me settled. We had dinner together and my mom was drinking wine, a lot of wine. Even Sandy noticed her own best friend was different. Deep down you could tell my mom was mad she didn't have full trust in Jake. She would make excuses to call him that whole day, she would pretend we had a car related question, or what kind of paint we should buy because we were going to paint my new room. Any chance she got to contact or text him she would. I am pretty sure he stopped replying after a certain time which put her on edge.

My Mom and I headed over to Sandy's father in laws house and before we got there, she stopped and got a bottle of wine. She was already noticeably buzzed and would snap at me at any given moment. All my childhood emotions started to come back, something I hadn't felt in over a year. I was anxious around her, scared of her… all over again. She was a different person, but the anger was familiar. I was texting Sandy letting her know that my mom was pretty drunk by this point. For some reason I felt the need to update her because my mom would snap at me loudly, my mom saw me texting and since I had put down the paint brush to do so, she got angry. She started screaming at me threatening to not help me anymore if all I was going to do was text. "I'm sorry, I was on my phone for two seconds." I replied. She raised her voice and had no problem being as loud as possible. "I don't need to fucking be here you ungrateful bitch." This was my first night at this man's house, I had only met him once before and this was happening. I am sure it was awkward for him to have a strange girl in his house as it was for me too. And here I was, night one and my mom is screaming at me in this house with thin walls. I was trembling,

"Mom please, please don't yell here." I begged. She didn't care, she continued to rip me apart with her words. I knew she wanted to just scream at me, so I quietly said, "Can we just sit in your car and finish this mom? I don't want him to hear this." I knew that if I had least complied to letting her scream at me, she would be happy to relocate.

We sat in her Toyota Sequoia outside the house, she is in the driver's seat, and I am in the passenger. My heart was pounding, I started to panic as I prayed he didn't hear anything. It took me back to a place of complete helplessness. My mom, screaming at me in the driver's seat made me think someone was going to call the cops. Then everything took a turn for the worst. Her screams were getting louder, I hardly remember what she was saying at this point because all I could do is look at the windows of the house hoping he wasn't looking through the blinds at this ridiculous scene, when I finally turned to her and said, "You're drunk!" I don't know what came over me, I said it with fear in my voice. I needed to say it, I wanted her to hear it, in hopes she'd recognize that all her dumb decisions she was making right now were ridiculous. This floored her, she instantly got defensive as she always does when someone says she is drunk. Before I knew it, she started screaming, "I'm going to fucking kill us, I'm going to fucking drive us off a cliff." She was stepping on the gas pedal over and over; I can still hear the stomp and release of the accelerator in my head. The car luckily wasn't started but the keys were in the ignition as she attempted to start the car. I screamed and cried loudly at this point. I didn't care who heard us I hoped someone did at this point, this was like something I had never seen before. My mom looked over and almost got a rise out of me being so terrified and screaming. Then, she took her fist and punched herself twice in the face. I let out a blood curling scream. I had my head pressing against the passenger window trying to be as far away from her without getting out of the car. The window felt cold on the back of my head, and I needed it. I needed something to remind me that I was here, I was actually seeing this, feeling this, witnessing this.

My mom gave herself a bloody nose, as I was trying to control my breathing. I blacked out after that, the next thing I remember was her laying in my bed next to me in my room. I went to the bathroom and secretly text Sandy. I told her my mom had punched herself twice in the face. Sandy was shocked, I still had a hard time admitting to myself this was real life. I went to sleep, sad, and confused. How could I ever see her differently after this? What kind of person throws a temper tantrum like that and punches themselves? I couldn't make any sense of it. When I woke up in the morning my mom was already awake. She was getting her things together and Sandy asked us to stop by her house before my mom headed back up to Tahoe. I looked at her, she had two black eyes. Not one, but two black eyes. "Mom, look at your face." I said in a calm, trembling tone. "You did this to me!" she snapped. "What? How dare you say that." I said, now furious at this point. How could she say that? How dare she! There would be no way I could ever punch that woman and live to tell the story. I was sick to my stomach. She continued as if that was no big deal. I feared her, not in fear of her hurting me- although, maybe, but I was in fear of her mentally. How did she punch herself in the nose and then look at me the next morning and say I did it? What kind of parent even does that to their own kid?

We both pulled up to Sandy's house, my mom had sunglasses on. Sandy comes up to us as we get out of the car, my mom already snapping at anyone who tried to talk to her when Sandy said, "Tinsley, why are you wearing sunglasses?" "What the fuck? Really Candi? You fucking had to talk shit about me?" she snaps. "Tinsley you have two black eyes." Sandy points out. My mom in true Tinsley form says, "Fuck you Sandy." An argument rose from there, it was brief, but my mom got in her car and peeled out of the driveway.

She never spoke to Sandy again. They had a friendship of over twenty years, and my mom never spoke to her again. My mom left a nasty voice message on her answering machine telling saying she was going to tell Sandy's husband about all her affairs. Whether Sandy did or didn't have an affair, it was just once again how dirty my mom fights. I was grateful for Sandy in that moment because no one would ever be brave enough to call my mom out, and she did that day. I wasn't sure what was going to happen to my mom and I after that. She had already gone a year with not speaking to me, so I knew she would have no problem doing it again, which hurt me a lot.

## Chapter Nineteen

As I got settled in Napa, to my surprise my mom would keep in touch. Instead of saying sorry for what she did that night she threatened to drive us off a cliff and punch herself, she would ask if I wanted an old painting of hers, or some sort of decoration. That was her "sorry." It was always her asking if I was hungry or wanted something material posing as her way of making it "go away."

I was hanging out with Gio here and there and he put me through hell. He did steroids and had anger issues. He flaked on me all the time. He would say he was going to come pick me up for dinner, I would get completely dolled up and ready, and he would never show. He would text me the next day with some excuse. And I would always forgive him. I didn't get it; I was so wrapped around this guy's finger I lost any and all self-respect.

I was losing my mind hearing rumors about the other girls he was sleeping with. There was no point to bring it up to him because he always told me what I wanted to hear. Meanwhile, I was getting phone calls from my friends in Tahoe telling me about how my mom got kicked out of a bar, and got in a bar fight with someone at another place. It was humiliated.

My mom, Caley and Jax were headed to Spicer's Lake, Ca for our annual camping trip with my mom's side of the family. My mom asked if I wanted to meet them there and she would bring JoJo. I was excited to see my dog and my family, we were unable to make the camping trip in the previous years due all our family drama, so I was excited to pick up where we left off. I drove up there and planned to stay two nights. As I got here, we got settled in as the sun started to set. We all sat around the campfire that night and we were all drinking. My cousin Chris was two years younger than me, and his friend and I were drinking beer after beer. We weren't twenty-one yet but our parents were letting us drink with them. My mom and I took a nasty shot of vodka with everyone. It was so nice to see my little brother and sister, I knew they were going through a lot seeing as they still lived with her part of the time. My sister was heartbroken with how our mom was, I could see it. My brother Tyler was a little more resilient. He was a boy and always stayed busy and wasn't as sensitive as my sister Caley and I were.

As it got late, my mom had Caley and Tyler sleeping in the tent. My mom was really drunk at this point, she was slurring her words and stumbling her way to the tent with Caley and Tyler. My cousin Chris and his friend and I sat in his tent and brought more beer. We didn't want to go to sleep just yet, we wanted to drink more and hangout. Suddenly, my cousin's tent rips open, and my mom is standing there with this look in her eye. "What the fuck are you doing?" she says to me, "What? We're hanging out?" I replied, extremely confused. "Get the fuck out, you're not sitting in here with two seventeen-year-old boys." She snaps. "What are you talking about

mom?" I said, embarrassed. "Were just hanging out Auntie Tinsley."
Chris says in my defense. "No, get the fuck out." My mom grabs my
arm and rips me out of the tent. I was mortified. She tried to make it
look like I was some pedophile. I was so upset, and so embarrassed.
She kept yelling at me about how I shouldn't be in a tent with two
seventeen-year-old boys over and over. All we wanted to do was drink
more, I was so uncomfortable with how she was making me feel, I felt
gross that she was trying to make it look like I was some sort of
predator. I burst into tears; I wasn't going to sleep in that tent with her.
I crawled into JoJo's dog kennel with her and curled up with her,
crying and holding my dog. I didn't care for a blanket, I didn't care to
sleep in my car, I just wanted to be with my dog.

I couldn't stop crying, I was mostly hurt by what my mom was
trying to make me look like. I was devastated by it to be honest. As I
sniffled nonstop my mom opened her tent and told me to get in. I was
almost relieved because JoJo and I had no space in that dog kennel for
the two of us, so I got up and went into the tent with my mom and my
siblings. As I laid down on the far side, Caley was next to me, then my
mom, then Tyler on the other end. As we were laying down, my mom
starts drunkenly rambling on about how we don't want her to be happy
and how Jed can "fuck off and die." Although he wasn't my dad, this
was my brother and sister's dad and it hurt them to hear her say this.
Jed was gathering information regarding the living situation at my
mom's rightfully so, and my brother and sister were honest with their
dad about what it was like over there. My mom of course took that as
no one wants to support her relationship with Jake. This was also true,
but she wouldn't stop drunkenly saying how we're all ungrateful and
get everything we want, and we don't want her to be happy. She
rambled on and on, when I heard Caley sniffle. My little sister was
lying next to me crying as our mom took great pleasure in continuing
her hurtful words. It killed me to feel her next to me as she wiped her
tears, my mom might've gotten away with doing that to me, but I
wasn't going to let her do it to my sister. I never defend myself against
my mom, but something powerful came over me as I heard Caley
sniffle one more time, I sat up abruptly and with full force said, "Shut
the fuck up!" before I knew it, my mom punched me. She punched me
so hard in the side of the head I literally saw stars, flashes of light were
all I could see for a moment. I have never been punched before in my
life, not even by Jed. As my head went down with the force of her fist,

64

I clenched my fist and swung back. Caley and Tyler screamed the loudest screams they could possibly make. As my mom and I exchanged blows, she managed to pull my hair keeping my head steady, I reached back trying to release her grip when suddenly, she bit my finger. I didn't feel anything up until that point, I was in such shock by the fists flying and my head swinging that I finally felt agonizing pain when she bit my finger. I screamed and screamed, she wouldn't release until our tent zipper flew open. We sat up and looked to see who it was. It was my great Aunt Vee and my mom's cousin Carter. My Aunt Vee was diagnosed with cancer and going through chemotherapy. I'll never forget seeing her without her wig for the first time. Everything went silent as I looked at my great Aunt Vee and cried, I wasn't crying about my mom, I was crying because I was so sad she had to see this, and seeing her with no hair made me wonder how this might be her last memory of my mom and I. I sat still when I felt a warm liquid slowly crawl down my face. I slowly raised my hand up to it and felt the side of my temple and touched it, I pulled my hand away to see blood covering my hand. My head was bleeding from multiple areas. I don't even remember how many times she punched me, but my fingernail was completely off. My own mother had bit my fingernail off.

The next morning, we woke up and everyone was silent. My family was disappointed, I was disappointed and embarrassed. My Aunt Vee looked at me and said, "Candi honey, you should take a dip in the lake and rinse off." I had dry blood all over my hair. I was quiet, I had no words I could possibly say. My mom chuckled and said, "Pretty sure she will never hit me again." As if she was proud of the number, she did on me. I couldn't believe the smirk she had on her face. "Why would you say that?" I asked her. My mom replies in a snappy manner, "You hit me first." "WHAT? No I didn't." I shouted. My blood was boiling, I looked at my sister and said, "Caley who hit who first?" Caley was nervous to answer and almost stuttered to get it out, "Um, well, mom, you hit Candi first, but then she hit you." My mom shook her head and said, "Welp, you shouldn't have been in a tent with two teenage boys." I couldn't believe her, that was her alibi? Really? I once again couldn't believe my own mother did this to me.

I grabbed my bathing suit and walked down to the cold lake. I didn't want to get in the water it was so cold, but I didn't want my

Aunt Vee to see the blood all over my hair anymore. I got in the water and shivered as I tried to wipe the blood off my hands first. My finger, missing a nail, and extremely bruised, it hurt as I tried to scrub my hands and arms. As I dunked under the cold water I came up for air. My head hurt, it was so tender I couldn't scrub my scalp or run my fingers through my hair to get the blood out. I was trying and crying as I tried to work through my hair. I looked over and saw my mom getting in the water with me. "Here, just dunk under and rub your hair under water." She said, offering to help me. "You need to go under and rub it out." She suggested. "It hurts." I quietly replied. I was scared to even say that worried she would get mad at me for saying it. She stayed there in the water for her version of support.

I tried my best to get cleaned up and hung around for a little bit. I decided to go back home to Napa. I couldn't stay there, and I just felt like my soul was broken. I hugged everyone good-bye, completely ashamed of everything that happened last night. I hugged my Aunt Vee good-bye with tears in my eyes. That was in fact the last memory she had of us.

Chapter Twenty

Back home in Napa I didn't dive right into school for Medical Assisting. I got a job as an Esthetician at Massage Envy. I did well for myself there and managed to get myself a cute apartment in Napa. Gio and I were finally official. We would go to the gym together and drink with our friends after, this was his routine. Gio was the alpha of the group. What Gio says goes. I hated being with him because all the girls loved him, and he loved them loving him. He wouldn't even be attracted to a girl, but he loved knowing they wanted him. My insecurities drove me crazy because every few weeks I'd look through his phone and find another girl he was talking to. I was never this insecure in my past relationships, this was new for me. And every single time I had a gut feeling, I was always right. I never had an urge to look and didn't find something. We would fight, and break up, then get back together. Anytime I would meet up with a girlfriend for dinner, he would blow up my phone or show up at the restaurant that I was at to interrupt my dinner. He was extremely controlling and jealous. It was toxic, and unhealthy.

One night we were driving home when we accused me of flirting with someone at a party. He started yelling at me saying, "I know you want him just admit it." "I don't Gio, I told you a million times." I declared. Gio grabbed his steering wheel and jerked it really quickly making my head hit the window on the passenger side. I looked over at him with my mouth wide open in complete shock he did that on purpose. "Aww did you hit your head Candi?" He said with a big smile on his face. I was speechless, I couldn't say a word in that moment. I don't know what made me madder, the fact that he did that, or laughing about it after. I had tears in my eyes because my boyfriend who cheated on me all the time, accused me of hitting on someone, and then made sure I was punished for it after. Where do we go from here?

We got back to my apartment and sat on the couch. Both of us were having a glass of wine when he continued to accuse me of wanting someone I didn't. Then his temper hit. He took my coffee table with the red wine on it and flipped the table over. Red wine spilled all over my brand-new apartment carpet. I cried right away because of the stains on the apartment floor, and quickly grabbed a towel. Then, there was a knock at the door, I opened it, and it was my building manager. She was an uptight woman who ran the place and happened to live right below me. She heard everything. I apologized profusely, as I stepped outside to talk to her. I didn't want her to see inside the apartment and all the fresh red wine stains everywhere. I had only been living there for two weeks and this was how my reputation as a tenant was starting. She was furious about the noise, and I then asked if she should call the police. "No, No, everything's fine. I am so sorry and it won't happen again." Here I was, lying for my toxic boyfriend. I walked back inside in tears, humiliated that I was "that girl" who had to lie to cover up what a jerk did. Gio had a towel and was cleaning up the stains when he grabbed me and hugged me. "I'm sorry babe." I looked up at him and smiled. I believed him, I felt like he really had remorse and it was going to be better after this. What was this feeling? I loved this; I loved him. I knew everything would be better after that. I told him I can't risk getting evicted from this place and this couldn't happen again. He reassured me that it wouldn't. As we laid in bed, we were holding hands, "I don't like fighting." I said softly. "Keeps it interesting." He said. I was waiting for him to say he was kidding, or crack a joke, but he was serious. He rolled over and went to sleep.

A few nights later we had a small group of friends over at my apartment to watch the UFC fights. I told everyone we couldn't be loud because the apartment manager lived right below me and listens to everything, I was already on thin ice. Gio was drunk and said, "Oh no noises? Like THIS!" And jumped in the air and slammed down on the ground. His friends laughed; I couldn't believe he disrespected me like that all just to show off to his friends. I walked in the kitchen upset, I talked to his friend Sam and started to say, "You guys don't get it, we already had an issue the other night, and he goes and does this." Gio walked in the kitchen and can see my irritated look on my face. I looked at him and said, "You and your friends can fucking leave." Gio goes, "Oh yeah?" and grabs the back of my head and slams me down to the ground. Sam saw it and said, "Aw come on Gio, don't do that." You could tell he was nervous as he said it seeing as no one would dare stand up to Gio. Gio walked away as if nothing happened. I slowly got up, and scared to make anymore issue over this, I knew if I continued with telling him and everyone to leave, Gio would do something even worse. The thing about Gio, is he didn't care who was around, if he wanted to hurt someone, he would. And his friends never really stood against him because they feared him. That was my boyfriend.

As time went on, the more toxic things got. It was almost like we had a system of fighting, screaming, then making up. For some reason I just stayed. Gio ended up convincing me to move in with him at his mom's house. I was having trouble affording the rent, and my six-month lease was up. I loved Gio's mom, she was a kind, caring woman, a nurse. She was a single mom who raised Gio and his little sister Lilly. Lilly was the opposite of Gio. She was a straight A student, quiet, and driven. Gio was the rebel and a troublemaker. He stressed his poor mom out. Gio's dad had an affair on his mom years prior, and it completely crushed her. Moving in with them wasn't the greatest because Gio would start fights with me at her house and she would hear it all. She was an amazing woman, but a gentle parent. She never intervened and he would put hands on me more often now that he knew I would be homeless without him.

Gio cheated on me all the time but would never admit to it. I was in this sick vicious cycle where I knew the truth, but almost hoped he'd deny it. It killed me wanting to know the truth, but I also needed him to lie, for me to stay. I was lost, I was angry, I was losing myself. One night, Gio and I were at a party at our friend's house when I found out he hooked up with yet another girl. I couldn't hold it in any longer, I knew his friends all knew what he was doing and almost laughed about how stupid I was. Even their girlfriends knew all the things he was doing behind my back and allowed me to look like a fool. The girlfriend's had their boyfriend's back, which was having Gio's back. I was fighting this battle alone, per usual. I told him I was done, and wanted things to end and told him I was going to move out. We got in my car, and he was going to drive us back to his house but didn't take us home. He was continuously yelling at me and saying, "you're not leaving me Candi. Do you realize no one is going to want you after me? I would fucking kill anyone you tried to fucking date." I was crying and screaming at him, furious, broken, and betrayed. I was almost used to him betraying me, I was mostly hurt about the girls I had considered my friends who knew about all these things and were sometimes present for it. I was beside myself and couldn't take it anymore. Gio drove my car up this dark long road. I was screaming and so was he, I had a feeling he was going to kill me. I without hesitating jumped out of the car when it came to a stop and starting sprinting as fast as I could. I had no idea where I was, it was pitch black and I was desperate to find a house to run to. Before I knew it, Gio was right behind me and grabbed me. I can't even remember how he got me back in the car because I was kicking and screaming for my life.

The next thing I knew, Gio turned down a road that only faced a vineyard. It was a road that wasn't visible to anyone passing by, not to mention it was after midnight. I was in the passenger seat when he grabbed my head and put me in a headlock. It felt like it took no strength for him to hold me still as I was scratching and trying to pull his arms away so I could get a gasp of air. Everything seemed silent although I knew I was screaming, it almost felt as if everything was slow motion. I couldn't even hear myself scream and all I remember is sensing how calm he was as he was tightening his arms around my neck. Gio trained in Jiu Jit sui and mixed martial arts fighting, he loved UFC, and knew every single move. He was taking pride in his grip, it was beyond killing me for him, it was his ego within being proud of his own training. It felt almost as if it was a dream, I remember looking around with my eyes, blacking out with glimpses of the stars in the sky, the steering wheel, and his leg. It was like my eyes scanned and would lose their course. I am not sure how I got so lucky being to petite, and where my strength came from in that moment, but while being held steady by my neck, I started kicking the passenger window repeatedly. And then it shattered. I remember hearing the noise of the shatter as I kicked it. Gio released me, not because he wanted to, but because he was shocked, he was not used to me acting out in such a way. The loud sound of the window startled him.

Gio took us back home. I was too shaken up to even address if I was injured. He apologized, kissed me and held me as we fell asleep. For some sick reason it was almost as it I craved the "I'm sorry" moments so much because I finally felt loved or needed. It was this feeling of affection that I wanted. As we woke up in the morning he held and kissed me again. I had tears in my eyes when I looked at him. Geo ran his fingers through my hair. I was empty inside. I didn't even know who I was anymore.

I got up and went to the bathroom and looked in the mirror. Tears rolled down my face uncontrollably, I had a huge painful bump on my head and my wrist was hurting, but neither of those things were why I was crying. It was the bruising all around my neck. My entire neck was officially bruised. This hit me harder than any other mark I had, this reminded me that he tried to kill me. That I could have died. And here I was, still with him.

Chapter Twenty-One

Gio and I decided to move into a townhouse together just the two of us, a family friend of mine Maggie, was planning on selling it but offered to rent it to us until then. It was in this adorable quiet complex. Seeing how quiet and well-kept it was instantly stressed me out. I hated how much it worried me knowing Gio didn't respect a noise ordinance, neighbors, or even my own family friend's property. He loved to entertain and have his buddies over to drink, it was never mellow. It was constant beer bong, drunken boxing, steroid injections with his friends every day. That townhouse never felt like home to me, it was a party house for Gio and his friends.

I was constantly stressed. I hated being at work because I knew he was doing something disloyal. I was still working at the Spa, and he was selling pot. Gio was so good looking that girls would constantly buy from him in hopes to see him or smoke with him. He loved attention and flirting with anyone just for simple reassurance that he was constantly desired. Gio was in the shower one night when I had an urge to look through his phone, I slowly crept into the bathroom and looked in his pants lying on the floor. I quietly searched the pockets and to my surprise it wasn't there. He hid it, on purpose during his shower. This was easy confirmation he was hiding something. Something instantly came over me and told me to look in his underwear drawer, I have never thought to do this before, and it was almost like God was constantly giving me signs. Anytime I ever found anything out about Gio, it almost fell into my lap. I never snooped due to insecurity, but proof would just come to me. God was showing me red flags left and right.

I slowly opened his underwear drawer and there it was with a blinking red light which was an indication of a text message notification. I was shaking as I opened the messages. The text read, "I loved kissing you today." I couldn't even control my thumb as it was trying to scroll back to see the number so I could call it. The shower turned off, and I could barely breath. Yet again, he is doing this and after I got us a place to live and let him use my car every day. He got out of the shower and walked in the room and saw me holding his phone. "Fuck you." I said. He ripped the phone out of my hand. "Who is she? Who is she?" I yelled repeatedly. I don't even know why it even mattered who it was anymore, he was the problem. The fight continued as I walked into the kitchen, he followed me out there. Denying all of it, "it's nothing, it's nothing." He replied stupidly. "Fuck you I am done, I deserve so much better." I screamed and I grabbed my phone running back into the room shutting and locking the door. Gio started to flip out, accusing me of being in the room and texting "my other boyfriend." Before I knew it, he broke the bedroom door completely in half. It wasn't even like he barged though it. He completely snapped the door in half.

I was sitting on my bed with my phone in my hand and he jumped to wrestle me for it. There had been countless times he's taken my phone so I couldn't text my friends or call for help. I was not going to let him win this time. I tried with all my might to keep him from getting my phone when he lifted me and shoved me across the room. I quickly got up and tried to grab my phone out of his hand, he kept pushing me back as we were screaming at each other. I finally said something in hopes to hurt him and yelled, "I am going to fuck someone else. You get to, so now I will too." I've never threatened this before and didn't even care what was going to happen next.

Within the blink of an eye, he was straddled on top of me holding both my hands over my head hitting the side of my head repeatedly. I was screaming and crying begging him to stop. I couldn't even feel each hit because I was in such shock. I felt like this was the time he was going to get away with killing me. Warm blood started to move down my forehead, I remembered how this felt. Gio was in such a rage and on a cycle of steroids, he paused to see the blood. He yelled out loud with a smile on his face as if he was getting pumped with excitement and bent down and licked the blood off my face. I was screaming even louder now in bigger fear, not of death at this point, more so of wondering what kind of monster this was. He continued to lick all around my face with my arms still being held above my head I started to panic, shaking my head back and forth when suddenly I bit his tongue. He yelled in pain and gave me one last hard smack across my face when I saw a flashlight and a loud bang on our back sliding glass door of the master bedroom. He released me and I immediately ran to the door. Five police officers with flashlights staring at me. "Help me." I cried. I could hardly make the words out.

Gio was arrested, and I chose not to press charges. Although, the court system and district attorney choose to press their own. The next morning, I woke up, alone and confused from all that had transpired the night before. The bedroom door was in pieces, the room was a mess, and then I looked in the mirror. I could hardly notice the bruises because my left eye was beet red. It wasn't red like a black eye was forming, it was my actual eyeball. The entire eyeball was bloody. When someone has blunted force trauma to their head or temple it can rupture some of the blood vessels in your eye. I looked like a sad zombie, and I had to call into work, I couldn't let anyone see my face like this.

My phone rings and it was a call from the county jail, it was Gio. I answered, I was pathetically excited he was calling. "Hello?" I said nervously, "Babe." Gio said, he sounded weird. I started crying, I felt so bad he was in jail, and I just wanted to hug him. I hated how weak and toxic we were. "I love you." Gio said, "I love you too." I replied with relief. "You almost bit my tongue off." He said with a slight chuckle. "Well, you licked my face like a psycho." I snapped back. I was defensive because I wasn't going to act like I should be sorry for that. No one could even access anyone's tongue like that unless they were kissing which was definitely not the case. "I know babe, I'm sorry. I'm over here sitting here in jail with a swollen fucking tongue. But I didn't call to fight. I am limited on time, and I just want you to know I love you." He said. "Okay, I love you too." I hang up the phone and sit down for a minute. Feeling stupid, and guilty. I felt so disappointed in myself for wanting to be back together with him, knowing this was never going to get better.

I wanted to end it but couldn't at the same time. I loved him, and wanted to be with Gio but didn't know where to go from here. No matter what the circumstance was with Gio and I, I knew going back home to my mom's was worse. At least Gio was sorry for hurting me when he did, my mom was never sorry. I was officially in an abusive relationship.

# Chapter Twenty-Two

Gio was released from jail, and we were back at our normal routine. Romance, gym, arguing. The hardest part was going out in public with people knowing about how toxic our relationship was. I felt like people would just stare at me like I was either stupid or equally psycho. And they were right, I was both. I was stupid for staying with him, a cheater, a liar, and a woman beater. And I was psycho for fighting back at this point, he'd hit me, and I'd hit him back. It wasn't right.

A couple weeks later my family friend Maggie called me and told me we needed to move out. The neighbors had all been complaining about the parties, the loudness, and hearing the fights between Gio and I. I was devasted, not so much about how we needed to move out, but by disappointing Maggie and for disrespecting her place. I felt terrible, had I lived there alone this would have never been an issue. Gio had ruined yet another roof over my head. We had to move back in with his mom. I am sure she dreaded that too. She and I had a great relationship, she knew how Gio was and the issues he had. But our toxicity disrupted her household at times, so she certainly wasn't jumping with joy to have us move back in together.

Gio and I decided to take a trip up to Tahoe. We wanted to give his mom some space and hoped for a little trip for him and I to get back on track as a couple. Gio loved to drink, and he loved to drink and drive. I didn't know anything different since he did it all the time. We went to the beach and drank all day, then went back to my mom's. My mom and Jake were drinking per usual, and Jake was coming across as very confrontational with Gio. Gio normally would be willing to fight anyone but surprisingly was the bigger person when it came to Jake. Gio and I decided to drive home back to Napa and not stay the night at my mom's. It was still early evening, around five o'clock pm, when we were barely out of town when I saw that Gio received a text from a girl. It was an inappropriate photo of her to him. I was pissed, "Pull over!" I said, I just wanted out of the car. I couldn't be near him any further. He refused to pull over when I started screaming, "Pull the fuck over, I am done with you!" He pulled over. I got out of the car and started walking, I was going to head straight back to my terrible mom's. I couldn't even decide which was worse, but I needed to be alone. Gio went to grab me to pull me back in the car, and that's when I knew he was angry now too. I knew going back in the car meant he was going to hurt me for making him chase me down the road. I reached back and smacked his shoulder. Right as I did that, an undercover police officer just so happened to be driving by. He pulled over and called two more officers over. I was arrested for battery that day. I was crying, mad that we could've stayed at my mom's but couldn't because Jake can't refrain from fighting, mad that Gio yet again had been cheating on me, and mad that I was arrested when I didn't even hit Gio in the face like he deserved. I was booked in the county jail and cried for two hours when my mom bailed me out. It was almost like I did her proud by being a fellow fuck up. That's the only time she was there for me, when I made a trashy, immature decisions. God forbid I was ever trying to something good for my life she wanted no part of it. It was like she wanted me to do okay, but never better than her. I was grateful she bailed me out and Gio was waiting at my mom's to comfort me. It was such a toxic relationship yet Gio and I both knew that we would never leave each other or judge each other. He was all I really had.

We headed home the next day; I had a court date ahead of me within a couple weeks. As the time came for me to appear in court, it was understood that the charges would be dropped. I was so grateful I didn't have this charge over my head and on my record. I promised myself to never act like that again. I am so grateful for that experience because it showed me there are truly consequences for your actions. I couldn't continue to be in a physically violent relationship, this was going to cost me so much more than I thought. But I needed him, as a security blanket. I had nowhere to go, nowhere to stay. He was able to get away with it all, especially since he knew how toxic my alternative was. He held that over my head at any given moment.

One night we were hanging out with our friends when I got a message from someone I knew from Tahoe, telling me my mom had just gotten in a fist fight with a girl I went to high school with. I immediately called my mom; she was belligerent and hysterical and hardly making any sense. "Mom what happened"? I asked, "Find out where Allison lives!" she yells. "What? Allison? Allison who?" I am confused, she clearly wanted revenge on the girl she got in a fight with. My mom hung up on me, she scared me with this rage because when she sees red there's no stopping her. I started making phone calls and getting more information, I wasn't trying to find out where this "Allison" lived, I wasn't going to partake in my mom's quest to potentially do something highly illegal, but I was trying to figure out what really happened. Come to find out Jake was cheating on my mom with a girl I went to high school with, Allison. And my mom found out where they were, went to their house and tried to fight her. She apparently brought a bat. My mom started swinging, drunk and out of control when Allison's friend Tara finally punched my mom in the nose, breaking her nose. I called Jake and started screaming at him when he said, "Your mom is a drunk crazy bitch who came over here with a bat and started fighting everyone." "Then stay the fuck away from her!" I yelled. I couldn't believe my mom was acting like this. I didn't expect much from her, but she was clearly losing herself to a point where she was going to end up hurt or in jail.

A few weeks had passed when she was back with Jake. My mom had to get rhinoplasty done on her broken nose. And as her and Jake rekindled, she bought him a truck. He was in need of a vehicle, so she offered to take him to the dealership and buy him a truck. What the hell was wrong with her? And to make matters worse Jake was getting evicted from his place, so he moved in with my mom. This was getting out of hand. He was now officially living with my mom, in our house. After some girl just broke her nose because of him. I had enough of my own problems with Gio to even get myself to get too emotionally invested in what she was doing, but what angered me was the fact that she partied hard with Jake, allows his friends over, and my little brother and sister lived there too. Not to mention, Jake was selling weed.

I continued to hear about awful stories about my mom and Jake being at parties and bars that my friends were at, and Jake and her always ending up in a fight. Either with someone else, or each other. Jake loved to fight; he loved the idea of knocking someone out whenever he could. I remember him bragging about all the street fights he's been in and how he would win all of them. I always thought it was the most unattractive and immature thing in the world to brag about such things, and that was who my mom was dating.

I got a phone call one day and it was Jed. I missed him, I missed my mom being with him, they were never "in love" and they weren't a good example, but my mom was a completely different person now because of her obsession with Jake. Jed and I chatted for a bit because he was ready to fight for full custody now that she moved Jake into her house. Caley had come home to her dad's after being at my mom's and told him about all the unruly things going on there, as well as our fist fight from camping. I don't blame Jed for taking this action. He asked me about what I knew about Jake, and I didn't hold back on my opinion and the stories that I heard, Jed heard the same stories. Tahoe is a small town, and it wasn't hard to get a few statements from outsiders. It's not that I wanted my mom to lose custody, I wanted Jake to be forced to move out at least.

Weeks later I found out that Gio had been cheating on me while we were at a party. The girl he cheated on me with was at the party we were at as well. I was done, I was sick of looking like a fool, I was sick of being the only girl in the room who didn't know what was going on, I couldn't do this anymore. I called my mom and told her I needed to move home. She told me I could. I packed my clothes and headed back home to Tahoe. I couldn't even give my work notice, I had to get out of there. I had nowhere else to go. I even called Jed to let him know my situation. I was not ready to move into my mom's house with this new lifestyle she morphed into.

As I got settled in my room, I was so happy to be back with JoJo. She was my everything, she never left my side ever. It didn't matter where I went, she was there. It was no secret how much my dog meant to me, everyone knew my love for her and her love for me. It was bizarre living there, my mom and Jake sitting on the couch drinking whiskey, then going out to the bars, they'd bring a bunch of Jake's friends back to party after. Our house was loud and disrespected by many. It felt like I lived with a bunch of college roommates. Meanwhile Gio was trying to get me back, I was sad leaving him. I missed him so much and I was spinning out of control wondering who the hell he was probably sleeping with now. The thing about Gio, is he couldn't stay loyal to me, but he didn't want to lose me.

My mom and Jake built another room in our house. He did the shittiest job ever, this house that I literally helped build was now being remodeled in the cheapest way possible. My mom and Jake added the bedroom for Jake's son to move into. He was getting out of juvenile hall. Great, just great, now I must live with this punk. My life felt like trash. After I would come home from being at work as a bartender at the Moose Lodge, or seeing my friends, I would notice Jake's son had gone through my belongings. He had stolen one of my Tiffany's necklaces that Gio got me, and I could tell he rummaged through my drawers to see if I had any valuables stashed somewhere. I am extremely OCD, and I could tell if something was even slightly moved.

I told my mom that I knew Jake's son had gone through my drawers and my necklace was stolen. My mom decided to help me out by getting a lock for my door. This was ridiculous, I, in my own home had to have a lock on my bedroom door to keep some ungrateful, pot smoking kid from stealing from me. What a complete joke. There was no questioning him, or anything. She just let him be him, because she wanted to be the greatest mother figure in Jake's eyes. If I did that to anyone, my mom would light me up. Jake's son would bounce back and forth between his dysfunctional mom's and our house. He was always up to no good and I hated our household because of it.

One night I went out to one of the bars that my mom and Jake went to often. This was a bar that I would never go to with my friends, it was dirty, and divey. Typically, people with no real job went there, and my mom and Jake were frequent flyers, not to mention she had been eighty-sixed from the other dive bar they liked to go to for getting in a fight with a woman over a pool table. Once again, humiliating. My mom went from being this toxic yet busy mom who shuttled her kids around from sport to sport, having a six-figure job at the hospital, to a bar hopping, beer drinking, fist fighting trash of a woman. I invited one of my friend's Jessica, to come along with me, my mom was a partier now and I was broke, so if I wanted to go out, and at least have my beer paid for, we had to go with her. Jake was at another bar that night and my mom would always make it a point to be out drinking too if he was doing the same in attempt to make him jealous. My mom walked in as if she owned the place, as if she had her "regular" pals there who again were about half her age. You could tell the bartenders were used to her being there, but not excited. As I am sure she has acted out and made scenes there as well. My mom was playing pool as Jessica and I sat at the bar when the bartender asked me, "Is that your mom?" "Yes" I replied with a slight shrug. "She's a wild one, isn't she?" I added trying to lighten connection. "She sure is." The bartender said, in an annoyed tone. He was certainly no stranger to her antics.

A few moments later, I heard someone say my name, so I gazed over my shoulder. It was Allison, the one that both Jessica and I knew and went to high school with, the one that slept with Joe, the one whose friend broke my mom's nose. She was excited to see me as if we were besties and went to hug me, I was slightly caught off guard considering I had sent her a rather harsh Facebook message the night of the incident. Right as her arm was reaching in for a hug my mom darts like the speed of lightening and shoves her. "Oh hell no you fucking bitch, you won't be fucking hugging my daughter." She yells. "Tinsley, I don't want any issues." Allison said backing up. "Fuck that" my mom continued; she was ready for a fight, and before I knew it Allison took off, which was smart because my mom is not the one you want to fight. The bartender, without missing a beat immediately called the cops. I think he was hoping for something to happen so he could get rid of my mom. As the cops were on their way, I told my mom he had called the police, and she quickly took off out the back door. She took off so fast, Jessica and I couldn't even find her. Jessica and I got a ride home as I was repeatedly calling my mom trying to find her, she wasn't answering, and I was worried. I finally had to call Jake and tell him what happened so that he could help find her.

My mom ended up running to another bar and calling her friend to come pick her up. I was at home with Jessica just completely embarrassed and annoyed by the whole situation. Jessica was not surprised at all; she had partied with Jake and his buddies before and knew all too well what my mom had become. I knew there was no way I could go out with my mom again; I looked just as bad as she did walking into a place with her. Ever since I was little, I hated scenes, and constantly felt judged, because of my mom. People say you shouldn't care what other's think about you, but I did. I was mortified by how my mom functioned and I wanted no part of it. It wasn't so much about being judged by others, it was more so about how I chose to conduct myself, and my own mother did it poorly. It was difficult to be around someone who put energy into finding conflict anywhere she went. I was always agitated when I was with her because I was on high alert.

## Chapter Twenty-Three

Things started to unravel rather quickly. I was missing Gio, and mostly because I was unhappy about my home life. I was keeping up with my college classes that I was taking to become a medical assistant. I was doing well in school for once. Jed and I talked more and more; I would call him for advice on many things. He knew how my mom was and often helped give me validation that she was not mentally stable. He was able to get a court order that if Jake was present at my mom's address, then she could not have Caley and Tyler there. My mom was livid, she was seeing red that "Jed was out to get her" in her eyes. She claimed it was always control and power that he wanted, but if I was a parent, I wouldn't want my kids in a household like that either. My mom was in tears in the kitchen knowing that Jake was considering moving out, I was sitting at the table eating cereal when my mom looked at Jake and said, "let's just move somewhere together." I dropped my spoon in my bowl, completely sick to my stomach she asked him this. Move? With him? And just forget about Caley and Tyler I thought to myself. I was a legal adult, and my mom didn't like me, I was used to that. But she loved Caley and Tyler, and they loved her, how could she do that to them? Jake looked at her and said, "We can't right now babe." He wasn't saying that out of the kindness of his heart though, he had other reasons why he didn't want to move away, he was still secretly sleeping with Allison.

My mom was so desperate to keep Jake in her life that she went and rented another house. A dark, dingey, rundown home with a sloppy landlord. So, we had our house, and then a house for Jake. Her plan was to fix up the house and to move in there with him considering the court order was specific to Jake not being allowed at the address of our current residence. She was paying Jake for all the labor. I couldn't believe it, yet again, how much she was willing to do for him, but wasn't even willing to help me pay for my college books without holding it over my head. She had Jake stay at the other house during the days she had Caley and Tyler, and then he stayed with us when they weren't there.

My mom drank and partied more and more. It wasn't so much that she was genuinely numbing herself, it was that she was constantly trying to keep up with Jake and his lifestyle. She needed to prove that there was no other woman that could keep up and fund his way of living. She knew her money is what held them together, she needed him to need her or else she knew he would be long gone.

One night I had a few friends come up to visit me from Napa, we went out to the casinos and then ended up back home later. My mom and Jake were doing their usual bar hopping and weren't even home yet, it was about midnight when Jake stumbled in my mom's house. "Where's my mom?" I asked, confused. "She got arrested." He said. "What!" I yelled. "She got a DUI." He replied. "What the hell? How?" Jake then proceeded to tell me that they were driving with a handle of whiskey in the car when there were some jay walkers leaving a bar. Apparently, my mom and Jake, who were both intoxicated yelled and cursed at the jaywalkers. The group of people yelled back, making my mom and Jake both happy to pull over and continue with an altercation. My mom got out of the car trying to fight the group of people when the cops came. My mom was resisting arrest, drunk and disorderly. When the officers arrived on scene, my mom was disorderly, and resisting arrest. She was booked and went to jail.

Jake was laying on the couch when the house phone rang. The caller ID read "El Dorado County Corrections." "Mom! Are you okay?" I said worried, I wanted to hug her, I knew she was out of control, but hearing my own mother was in jail made me want to comfort and protect her. "Fuck you! Let me talk to Jake!" She yelled. "What the hell?" I replied, confused, "Put Jake on the fucking phone." She screamed. I was offended but also knew she was belligerent and angry about her situation. I handed the phone to Jake, where she cried to him, I could hear how sweet and vulnerable she was with him on the phone which hurt more. I was nothing but an inconvenience to her, always.

The next day she was released and extremely pissed off. She knew this would affect her custody battle as well. A DUI is public knowledge, not to mention, every cop in town knew my stepdad. I remember watching her talk to Jake blaming everyone but herself for her actions. She had zero accountability for what took place. "How could you be so stupid? If you act that crazy when you're drunk, maybe you shouldn't drink." I wanted to say to her. It was a pretty simple solution to see that alcohol was the absolute common denominator to all her problems.

Jed didn't have a hard time building his case against her with all these documented incidents. But it took time for the courts to set up a court date and for my mom to prepare her defense. It was the Fourth on July when I wanted to go to the beach and meet some friends. I was always really strict with myself about not drinking and driving, not because of what my mom had gone through, but because I knew it wasn't worth the risk. Jake had other plans for the fourth of July that didn't include my mom. He did this often, she hated that she couldn't keep tabs on him, even if he lived under both her roofs. Deep down she knew that he had secrets which is why she tried everything she could to provide a life for him that he couldn't leave. My mom said she wanted to come to the beach with me, and that she would drive. I didn't want her to come, but I felt bad for her being alone and stranded by herself all day while her boyfriend was excluding her. I allowed her to come with.

We got to the beach, and I chatted with some of my friends. My mom was drinking but I figured it was okay if she just had a few beers with us. I was shocked she was even allowing herself to do that seeing as she just got a DUI. This beach was a known party beach, and it gets rowdy. My mom was noticeably drunk at this point, she was stumbling around and taking shots with kids even younger than me. I watched her smoke a blunt with someone, I knew it was time for us to go. She was getting a confrontational look in her eye. Before I knew it, she was yelling at a group of girls, they looked confused and clearly didn't want to fight and I think they were more shocked that a grown woman was not only at this beach but cussing them out. I told my mom that we should leave, so we loaded up and drove home. She was drunk, and I was buzzed but I was not about to offer to drive. I told her we should get a cab and she was immediately offended, even if I slightly hinted that she wasn't in a position to drive, it was a fight. We were driving home through the casino strip when we were stuck in typical fourth of July traffic. There was a party bus in the lane next to us full of guys. They cheered and yelled to us. We both laughed and I waved when suddenly, my mom rips up her bikini top and flashes her bare breasts at the bus full of guys. I was mortified. "Mom what the fuck?" I said, I couldn't even fake my embarrassment. "What! They're just tits!" She screams, with the windows down. "That's not classy mom." I said hesitantly. Not that I was all high and mighty, but that in my eyes was just trashy. My mom freaked out, I had clearly offended her. "You fucking prude, you fucking prude bitch!" She continued to scream at me. I wasn't giving in; I wasn't about to say sorry which is what she wanted. This angered her even further when suddenly, she slammed on the brakes and threw the car into park on the highway and hopped out. She flipped me off and screamed at me as I sat frozen in the passenger seat. "What the fuck am I supposed to do?" I yelled to her from the passenger window as she walked off flipping in a bikini top me off. Everyone was watching, we were stopped at the heart of party central outside the casinos, people bar hopping, walking around, cars were honking behind me as the parked car was now holding up traffic. I was worried someone was going to call the cops, although I had done nothing illegal, I was not ready for a scene caused by my mom with both of us being in bikinis. I quickly jumped over to the driver's seat and threw the car in drive. I drove home, without her. I called Jake to let him know what happened, if she was going to listen to anyone it was going to be him, and I wasn't willing to keep the part out about her flashing a bus full of guys either. I hated her because of him, she was completely acting out like a troubled child in school because they have a shitty home life. And I no longer felt sorry for her.

Jake eventually found her, and they carried on about their party night. I called Jed crying, I vented to him over and over at this point I had nothing to lose. He was my closest confidant when it came to my mom. I went to sleep as soon as I got home, I was worried about what was going to happen later. Luckily at whatever hour my mom and Jake stumbled in, I am pretty sure she forgot about what happened, and or, didn't want to talk about it because she knew she was wrong. I was beginning to despise my mom and everything she stood for.

## Chapter Twenty-Four

. My mom had court where she was officially charged with a DUI. I am pretty sure there were other charges she was facing due to her behavior that night, but the issue was her place of work finding out. Human resources questioned about her charges, and this was a hospital that strived for a certain "standard" amongst their employees. Especially since my mom was pretty high up within the finance department, this wasn't a good look for her. My mom, once again, instead of being accountable, she was defensive for being questioned about her charges. Again, blaming Jed for "framing" her and trying to ruin her life. My mom quit her job, on the spot and told her boss, whom she had a long working relationship with to "Fuck off."

Now this was scary, my mom had lost her job which was the most irresponsible thing ever. And, not to mention, Jake knew this could compromise his lifestyle. His bills were paid with this woman, his son's bills were paid, his nice new truck had a monthly payment, he was not ready to have any of that compromised.

This is the night I will never forget, Christmas Eve, and a night I will never forgive my mom for. It hurts to write about this night as I think about it in detail. I was sleeping downstairs in my room with JoJo when my mom and Jake were upstairs drinking. They started getting louder, when I could hear him saying, "Your kids are all fucking ungrateful, you pay for all their shit, and they don't deserve shit." He was slurring his words, and my mom drunkenly says, "I know Jake, I know. They don't appreciate shit." He reiterates, "Fuck them, stop paying for them, ungrateful pieces of shit." I knew exactly what he was doing, he was putting it in her head to cut all of us off, so it was more money for him and his pocket. My mom didn't even pay my bills, all I did was live with her. She hadn't paid my bills since I was sixteen. How dare he even try to sacrifice the roof over my head, and to cut off my brother and sister who were now thirteen and fourteen. Luckily, they were at their dad's during this time, so it was just me. Jake's son was God knows where. As he continued to put it in her head about how awful her kids were and talking poorly about Caley and Tyler and how they run to their dad and tell them everything I got out of bed. I had had it. I walked up the stairs and said, "Shut the fuck up." My mom flies over the couch grabbing pictures off the glass table and started throwing them at me. I am crying and trying to block these glass frames me from hitting me while saying, "Mom, why are you letting him say this about us?" Jake stands up and charges over to me, he is huge, over six feet tall and the darkest look in his eyes when he says, "Get the fuck out of my house." "What?" I said, looking at my mom. Waiting for her to defend me. She agreed with him, "Get the fuck out." She yelled. My heart was pounding so hard I could hear it. "Fuck you Jake, this isn't your house, WE built this house!" I yelled back. Jake looked at me with a big smile on his face and said, "This is my fucking house, I'm the king of this castle." I looked at my mom with tears in my eyes. "Fuck you mom!" I cried and walked down the first block of stairs crying by the front door.

Jake was enjoying this power and wanted me out. He grabbed his phone and called the cops on me. He was on the phone with dispatch when he said, "This girl needs to get out of my house." He and my mom were both a whole landing of stairs away when he looked at me while holding the phone to his ear and said, "She's hitting me, she's slapping me!" As he proceeded to slap himself on the check repeatedly. I cried and looked at the two of them as if I saw a ghost. Was this really happening? He continued to smack himself. "I'm an entire landing of stairs away from you Jake you fucking liar!" I yelled. I could barely breath as I started to call Jed, I went to get my dog and some of my things. I was going to go over there. A police officer pulled up as I walked outside in tears, I told the officer what was happening and I said, "I just want to go to my stepdad's." The officer told me to wait by his car as I watched him walk up the stairs to the front door to speak to my mom and Jake. They both started yelling at the same time saying all sorts of things about me, when my mom said, "She slapped him." That moment right there made me sink. I have never hurt more in my entire life. How could she say that? How could she do that to me? She was right there. She knows I didn't! This could get me arrested. I stood there with JoJo next to me and watched as she continued with a lie that her boyfriend had made about me. I hate her. I could never forgive her for this.

The officer made his way back over to me, as I trembled with fear thinking I was going to be arrested for some sort of assault charge. The officer seemed all too aware with those two and how they operate. It was clear how intoxicated they were. I looked at the officer while crying and said, "Sir, I would never hit him because I know he would hit me back." That was true. How many times I fantasized about punching him and knocking him out seemed euphoric, but that garbage bag of a man would have no problem hitting me back. The officer believed me, I couldn't be more thankful for him. My little car was buried in the snow, and I couldn't dig it out to drive to my stepdads. The officer gave me and JoJo ride to Jed's house. Jed knew I was on my way with my frantic phone call to him during the incident. My sister by this time knew and was well aware of all that was going on. Her and I grabbed and hugged each other crying together for a moment, both sad that our mom is gone beyond repair, and this there is no saving her. I couldn't bring myself to tell her that our mom had even considered packing up and moving away with Jake.

I had called Gio and told him what had happened. He asked me to move back to Napa with him. The next day I had to have an officer escort me over to my mom's house as I shoveled my car out of the snow and packed my clothes. My mom's boyfriend Jake was yelling from the upstairs bedroom window saying, "She better not touch any of my shit, she can get her things and leave my house." I didn't react, as the officer yelled up to Jake and said, "She is getting her things and leaving, no need to cause more problems here." I was shaking as I was frantically trying to unbury my car as Jake continued to yell down and heckle me. The officer was shocked at how Jake was so comfortable yelling at me and him from the window.

I finally gathered my things and made my way back down to Napa to my shitty relationship. Jed was willing to keep my dog JoJo for me until I was able to get my own place and come back for her. I missed her so much already. I had given up on all my college classes without notice and just up and quit my life in Tahoe. I never felt like I had a real home, I had no safe place. My only safe place was with my cheating, beating, lying boyfriend. Although Jed let me stay with him the night my mom and Jake turned on me, he still wasn't my dad, I couldn't ask him to take me in. He wasn't even legally my stepdad anymore, he had no obligation to me, though I was grateful for him for being there for me.

As I got settled back in Napa yet again, I applied for a new job at an Aveda Salon. I was the front receptionist there and I was good at my job. I loved working there and the friends I made. Gio and I found a duplex for rent, we were so excited to try this again and move out of his mom's place, and I am sure she was just as thrilled. I was able to get JoJo from Jed as well. I finally had a place and JoJo could be with me too. Meanwhile, Jed had me write a statement regarding my mom and what type of mother she was. I was sick to my stomach giving this statement because I knew she could lose custody and she would likely hate me forever, but I hated her. I lost all respect for her for lying to that police officer for Jake. This wasn't a matter of revenge, because it pained me to participate in this, it was a matter of if this happened to my siblings, I know she wouldn't protect them either. Not to mention all the weird guys coming in and out of my mom's house and her and Jake selling weed, I just couldn't bear the thought of something happening to Caley and my mom lying to protect Jake and his friends. I needed to protect them, even if they didn't fully understand why.

I started having this repetitive nightmare, a vivid image of Jake taking a chainsaw to me and sawing my arm off, as my mom held me down. It brings me to tears to think about that dream even still. It felt so real and symbolized so much. The betrayal of the woman who is supposed to be my mother, the pleased look on his face while he did it, knowing he had won. They were perfect for each other. They were both ticking time bombs ready to detonate at any given moment. I was asked to appear in court, I had to drive up to Tahoe to sit in a court room and testify against my own mother. As I walked in to court my mom and Jake were sitting across the way. "My own daughter." She smirked. As if I should be ashamed of myself. Yet she was sitting next to the man that lied about me assaulting him which could have put me in jail. She should be ashamed. I felt weak, I felt nauseous, I felt defeated. There was no win in my eyes, I wasn't happy to be there against my own mother. She was a terrible mother, but she was still my mother. I wasn't close with my dad in the slightest. We would keep in touch and get lunch, but we weren't close.

As we sat in court, I was questioned about the fist fight my mom and I got in while we were camping. I hated reliving that moment, and seeing my mom have no remorse for it. She was against me in every single way, even before me testifying against her. When it was Jake's turn to come to the stand, they questioned him about the night of my mom's arrest when they got in a fight with the jaywalkers. The attorney questioned him and asked him why he felt the need to pull over and get in a fight with complete strangers, Jake slammed his hand down on the podium and yelled, "Cause I'm a man!" I couldn't believe my own eyes, I almost wanted to laugh at the fact that this guy couldn't even keep it together in the court room. As if this was some moment for him to show his dominance. I walked out of the court room; I couldn't take it anymore. I gave my statement and did my questioning, and I wasn't about to sit here and watch this monster that ruined my family continue with his lies and my mom to justify all her behavior. I got a call from Jed after as I was driving home, he had told me that they arrested my mom. She ended up acting out and was in contempt of court. They released her, but she was still handcuffed apparently. I few moments later I received a text from my mom's friend saying, "Shame on you." I was so angry; how dare she even say that to me when she has no idea what my mom has put me through. She only had my mom's back because my mom was willing to write a character witness for her when she went through a messy divorce and custody battle. The only difference was my mom's friend would do anything for her kids and loved them dearly. My mom lost full custody that day, because her relationship was more important.

As I got back to Napa, I went straight to Gio's mom's house, I met Gio there. It was an emotionally draining day. And Gio's mom told me that Jake had called and left a message on their answering machine saying that I had been giving blow jobs to multiple dudes during the time I was in Tahoe. Gio luckily didn't believe it, and this wasn't true in the slightest. Although Gio didn't deserve my loyalty, I still didn't hook up with anyone else. The fact that Jake had the audacity to call Go's mom's house and leave a message like that was ridiculous. My mom had been texting me left and right with anger, and then I text her telling her the voice message Jake left on Gio's mom's home phone. My mom wrote back and said, "Hmm, I don't see that he called that number when I looked through his phone." "Yeah mom, he DELETED that clearly." I text back. I sent her a picture of his phone number with the time he called on the caller ID. She never replied.

## Chapter Twenty-Five

A couple months had gone by, no contact with my mom and I was still in the same place with Gio. Our duplex was a constant party spot for him and his friends. I hated it, I was such a neat freak and such a clean person I was sick and tired of having to clean up constant liquor bottles and spills everywhere. Not to mention the constant fights Gio and I ended up getting in. Gio was on another cycle of steroids which meant an even bigger temper to deal with.

Gio and I were at a house party with some friends. Everyone was drinking and smoking, and Gio started to get in this mood like he was ready to fight anyone. If it wasn't me, it was someone else. We were getting ready to leave the party when a girl had winked at Gio, I saw it and questioned him about it. He of course denied she did it, and denied any connection with her, but I knew they were both hiding something, as I was getting ready to leave the party with him, I turned to her and said "Fuck you" out loud. I don't even know what came over me. I felt like I was acting like my mom. I felt like trash but at the same time I was going crazy with how many girls were so flattered by being Gio's dirty little secret. Gio was so good looking and muscular that girls would flock to him even if they knew their role was to be the side chick. It pissed me off how many girls lacked respect for another woman's relationship. As I said that to her, her boyfriend came up to me and said, "Wow, wow, wow" trying to calm me down as I walked away. Gio walked past me and up to the kid who said something, as if he was ready for this moment. Gio without any warning elbowed the kid in his face and was now top of him. I couldn't see what was happening because everyone circled around him trying to pry him off. He completely knocked this kid out, I thought he killed him. We left the party instantly and went straight home. We both knew what had happened was bad, this wasn't just a hit, the kid didn't even deserve it and I think Gio knew that deep down. His rage was out of control.

A couple nights later there was a knock at our door in the middle of the night, it was the cops. We let them come inside and they questioned us about the night of the incident. We each gave our statements, and they told us they would get back to us. Gio had put the kid in the hospital, and it ended his baseball career. I don't even know what Gio did to him specifically. I couldn't even bring myself to ask him because I didn't want to know, I felt terrible. I felt like this was all my fault to be honest. I should've never said anything to that girl. This resulted in completely ending someone's future with baseball. To this day it might be my biggest regret, I sent her a message on Facebook apologizing, she read it and never replied. I didn't care if she was fooling around with Gio at that point, I felt terrible for her boyfriend and didn't know what else to do.

A few days later there was a warrant issued for Gio's arrest. I had told Gio he needs to turn himself in. He refused at first, but I told him he needed to do what was right. It took some convincing but eventually he did. He was booked and was facing a hefty assault and battery charge. I was so embarrassed showing my face around town. I felt guilty, and then ashamed. I loved Gio, but I didn't agree with what he did and me being his girlfriend made it look as if I was his "ride or die." I wasn't. I might have let him get away with a lot for the things he did to me, but I couldn't stay by his side for doing this to an innocent person who didn't even want to fight Gio in the first place.

I would visit Gio in jail from time to time. A big part of me hated to admit it, but I almost liked him in jail. He couldn't cheat on me, there weren't parties at my house, he wasn't drinking or doing steroids. I loved it. My home life was peaceful, I'd workout at the gym, go to work, I'd get to see my girlfriend's, and had a clean house. I loved being able to see my girlfriends finally without Gio being able to blow up my phone or show up unannounced to drag me out of a restaurant like usual.

Gio ended up being granted work furlough. He was able to go to work and come back to jail. I found out that he was having some girl come meet him and bring him lunch while he was at work. This girl was a constant issue in our relationship, so it triggered me even more. She loved Gio and would do anything for him. She vandalized my car once when I called her from his phone a year prior, so for him to choose her, hurt me more. He could have chosen any other girl, but it had to be her. I decided to stop caring about questioning him. I wanted to get him back, I wasn't going to call him out because he was still paying for half our rent, otherwise I couldn't afford the duplex on my own. I decided to click into this spiteful gear, and it felt good. I was so sick of screaming and crying over always being cheated on I decided I was going to be a cheater myself. This was a dangerous and unhealthy mindset which was good for me. I didn't care at this point; I just wanted any sort of distraction other than feeling betrayed.

I became this dangerous, promiscuous vixen. For the first time in a long time, I felt like I was having a fun life. I was in a much better mood overall, which made me realize how much Gio brought me down. I slowly stopped answering his calls every night. One thing Gio hated was the thought of someone else being with his girl. He wanted to have his cake and eat it too. Word got back to him about another guy I was starting to hang out with. He called and questioned me about it, and I was honest, I just exploded with all the shit he's ever done to me and finding out what he was doing while on work furlough. I didn't even feel bad, I didn't feel one ounce of guilt. It had been almost three years of this roller coaster and I wanted off the ride. I went to sleep feeling fine at first, and then realized that this wasn't good. Now that Gio knew who it was I was hanging out with, Gio would make sure he paid for it.

Gio was getting ready to be released from jail when I told him he needed to stay with his mom for a while until we figure things out. I have no idea how he agreed to that, but he did. He wanted to work on things, but I also think he wanted to get back to his partying and smoking weed. I always had an issue with him smoking weed and I know he wanted to go straight back to the freedom of being able to do that. He couldn't get away with partying like that and living with me. One night I was home and I heard JoJo barking, there was someone in my backyard. I opened the back door to see who it was, but they took off. I know it was Gio. I wasn't even concerned it might be someone else, I knew it was him. I had been receiving text messages from him prior asking me where I was and what I was doing when they suddenly stopped. I couldn't handle this stress anymore.

I had confided in my friend Anthony about everything that was going on and told him I just wanted to be done with Gio and I was sick of my life with him. I told him I wanted to finally date and be treated like a princess for once. I wanted to be valued, respected, and desired. My friend Anthony was always brutally honest when he finally turned to me and said, "Candi, no one is ever going to date you here. They are all terrified of Gio. They want to date you, but they don't want to get their ass beat. Cause he will. He always will." That harsh reality hit me hard. He was right. I was never going to be able to break free from him.

Gio was still staying at his mom's yet was still helping me out with the rent. I had told him we were locked in a lease that I trusted to sign with him, so he needed to be a man and at least help me pay for his share because it's his fault our relationship went to shit. I was continuing with my normal routine, and work when I received a text message from Gio. It was a picture of his chest, he got a tattoo with my name on his chest. This was his attempt to win me back over. I thought he was an idiot, and I told him that. But I allowed him to come back home. I was flattered but still felt he was stupid for doing that.

We were both in this relationship full of secrets and lies yet couldn't stay away from each other. It was like fire meets fire with us. Although we were toxic, we still had this undeniable connection, we both loved fitness, we were both the life of the party, we could make each other laugh in so many ways, and he loved dogs. It was hard to stay with yet stay away from each other. Gio had told me he got a job painting houses with a guy who owned his own painting company. I was happy for him, and hoped this was a step in the right direction. The man who hired him was a recovering alcoholic, and I had told Gio that he needed to stop drinking prior to moving back in. I felt like this was a great opportunity for him and a good positive influence for him. Come to find out the man he was working with had relapsed, with Gio. I had a weird gut feeling one day after Gio came home from work one night and I looked in his car. I found a receipt from a liquor store of him purchasing a bottle of whiskey that day. I felt numb, it was almost like I couldn't even feel pain or sadness anymore. I decided to not react, I was done reacting, I felt like I'd rather just build my case against him and put a plan in place to leave him. I grabbed my phone and texted my mom.

Chapter Twenty-Six

I was broken, unhappy, and needed to get away. Those are the only situations my mom enjoys speaking to me, if I am not doing well. I don't recall if we ever spoke about what had happened in court months prior, but I had heard she and Jake weren't doing well so I think she was more willing to help me. I told her I needed to move home and told her everything about Gio. She offered to drive down and help me move. I was grateful for her in that moment, but depressed I was going back to Tahoe, and back to see Jake as well. Even if I could afford my own place in Napa, I couldn't escape Gio. He would show up anywhere I went. Anthony was right, every single guy I talked to would ask where Gio was at and would say they didn't want any problems. I needed to move. I was so sad, I was devasted to leave my job and my friends. I was now the Salon coordinator at my job and loved my coworkers. But I needed to get away.

A few days later my mom knocked on my door and I just cried to her. We hugged and gathered my things. Just as I was packing, I received a text message from a friend who sent me a picture of Gio with another girl at a party the night before. It broke me to see it, that kind of proof. It made my decision easier but pained me at the same time. I was really done this time and I knew it. I knew it couldn't do this back-and-forth thing anymore. The fact that I quit the job that I loved was enough for me to know that I needed to be done.

I headed up to Tahoe with JoJo. My mom followed me with her car full of my things as well. As we got to my mom's house, I opened the garage to start unloading my car. I looked over at a pile of things and saw my box of baseball cards with a piece of duct tape on it marked $10. Those baseball cards were given to me from my grandpa and my mom knew how much they meant to me. I didn't care to hold on to many sentimental items because my family was so small and so shitty, but my dad's dad Tony was an amazing grandpa and taught me how to play baseball when I was younger and I cherished those baseball cards. My mom knew how much those baseball cards meant to me. I looked over and said, "Why do my baseball cards have a $10 sticker on them?" "Oh, Jake and I had a garage sale last week." She said. "And you were going to sell my baseball cards?" I asked. "Well, you never took them." She snapped. In my head I was telling myself "No shit, because last time I had to pack my things I had to have a police escort. I didn't think I'd have to save my baseball cards from you and your boyfriend."
She was such a low person, but I was happy to be away from Gio, get back into school, and at least I had my dog with me. I was never going to leave her side; she was my rock.

About only a week had gone by when my mom found out Jake was still cheating on her with the Allison girl that was my age. My mom came rushing through the front door in the middle of the night holding her shoulder. "Mom! What's wrong?" I screamed trying to help her. She was holding her shoulder in pain. She proceeded to tell me that she found out where Allison lived and knew Jake was there, so she went to go steal the truck back from him that she bought him, and he ran outside and slammed her down to the ground. I fucking hated him. My mom didn't want to even address her pain, she was mad Jake was cheating and driving her truck that she was paying for. She succeeded in getting the truck back and was cussing him out on the phone telling him needed to move out. My mom went to bed and fell asleep, she had been drinking before she went over there to repo the truck. I heard sloppy, loud steps up to our front door, it was Jake. He didn't have a key to our house on him luckily and he banged on the front door. He was yelling at me as he saw me through the door window. "Open the fucking door, Candi." He yelled. I stood there frozen for a minute, terrified of him. I was genuinely scared; I slowly made my way back to my mom's room hoping she was still asleep. She was, she had a pill bottle of Ambien next to her. She was still breathing, "Oh good." I said to myself, she's passed out hard and won't be able to let him in. If she was awake, alert, and oriented she would have let him in. He continued to bang on the door, and this time he was pissed because roles were reversed now, he wasn't allowed in my house this time. He eventually left and I went to sleep, I pulled my dresser in front of my bedroom door so it couldn't be easily opened in case be broke in. I hardly slept that night because I was scared he would really kill me.

The next day my mom and I left the house as she told Jake he could go to the house and get his things and move out. She was mad and drinking beer even though it was only noon. She kept calling him every fifteen minutes to cuss him out. I, deep down was happy about this. I wanted her to hate him and to finally be done. Now she could fight for custody back and work on herself. When my mom and I finally came home after Jake grabbed his things, I noticed JoJo was incredibly sick. She couldn't keep anything down and couldn't eat or drink. She continued to throw up and I tried to make her rice, but she refused. This was sudden, she was fine when I left the house. I was planning to take her to the vet in the morning I was so concerned. I slept on the kitchen floor with her. I barely slept I was so worried. How could she get so sick out of no where? She didn't chew things; she never gets out and gets into mysterious things. What was going on?

Morning came and I brought her into the vet with my mom. The vet took an X-ray of JoJo's stomach and said he couldn't find any foreign body in her stomach. He said she was extremely sick for unknown reasons and the oldest nine-year-old German Shepherd he had ever seen. The vet looked at me and said, "Candi, I know this is hard, but I think you need to euthanize her." I couldn't believe this. This is not what I was expecting. Put my dog down? Now? How could I do this? Say goodbye to her forever? I dropped to my knees and cried and held her hugging her as hard as I could. I held her until her very last breath. My mom cried too. It was awful. The entire experience was awful. It wasn't peaceful at all, she struggled and fought for her very last breath. It was traumatic and didn't make sense.

As my mom and I got back home, I just sat on the couch and cried. My friend Jessica came over and brought me flowers. She knew how much JoJo meant to me; everyone knew. JoJo to me wasn't just a dog, she was my dog. My rock, the only thing who has ever loved me unconditionally. There is no other kind of love that could compare to a dog's love, I needed her just as much as she needed me. I couldn't wrap my brain around how she suddenly got sick like that. It wasn't until later that night that my mom sat next to me and said, "You know Candi, I am sure you don't want to hear this, but Jake really does feel bad JoJo passed away." I looked right at her; everything ran through my head in that moment. One, my mom was obviously still texting Jake, and clearly not sticking to her guns. But two, JoJo got suddenly sick the day he was at the house packing his things. He was here, alone with her. Jake knew how much my dog meant to me. It was no secret to anyone. I knew, with every muscle in my body that he poisoned her. He fucking poisoned her. "Jake killed her mom, Jake fucking poisoned her." I said with tears in my eyes as things started to click. "He wouldn't do that." My mom said in his defense. I didn't need to convince her, I knew it. And I couldn't even believe for one second that she didn't think he was capable of it.

My Birthday was in a few weeks, and I couldn't even look forward to it. Losing JoJo ripped my heart out and it was hard to feel happy again. The only positive in my life was that Jake was out of our house, but my mom was still secretly seeing him. She would have him go over to the other dark, dingy house she rented to help install new carpets and fix it up. She paid him of course. She was mad at him but would do anything to try and stay in contact with him, meaning making sure there was always work for him, she even tried to stay connected with him by helping him sell weed. What a joke all this was. My mom had poured so much money into him and with losing her job, she couldn't afford things as much as she used to. She ended up doing a "cash for keys" deal on our house. She sold it as is for a very small amount. We had basically lost our house, that we built. I was heartbreaking to have to move out. We had to move out within short notice and my mom was working at her new job, so I was left to do it all. That was the most torturous day ever, it was exhausting, and I did it to help my mom. I wanted to impress her by how hard I worked and how I wanted to make sure she had very little to do. I had met a guy a few weeks prior who I really liked, Dane. He helped me that day, it was a lot of work and completely went unnoticed. If you think about it, my mom, Caley, Tyler, and I all occupying the house for over six years, plus all the misfits my mom allowed in our house, it was a lot of work.

When my mom came home from work, there was no appreciation or thank you. I found myself exhausting myself trying to impress her by doing favors for her or helping her out. She had the worst luck with cars, she never stayed on top of the required maintenance for her vehicles and twice in one year she called me broken down on the side of the highway. Both times, Dane and I would come pick her up and help her out.

All my mom seemed to care about was maintaining her connection with Jake and then getting Caley and Tyler back home now that he was no longer there, which I agreed with now that our living situation was different. The house was three bedrooms, so my mom had a room, Tyler had a room, and Caley and I shared a room. Caley decided to mostly stay at her dad's but would come spend time with us often. Tyler enjoyed staying at our mom's mostly because she wasn't as strict as Jed. It felt good to have us all back together, but our house just never felt like home. You could tell Caley and I mostly missed our house, Tyler kind of just went with the flow with things, he wasn't as sensitive and his sisters. Caley and Tyler were high schoolers now, they were busy, and Caley had her driver's license. Tyler was an excellent wrestler, and Caley played soccer like me, but it wasn't really her sport, she was a good kid, she was excelling academically and wanted to go into nursing after high school. I was so proud of her. Caley and Tyler were both so lucky to have the option to go to college.

Tyler didn't care much for his studies, but loved wrestling and was planning to go far with that, he had no intertest in college. I remember being so envious of them that between my mom and Jed, they were supported. From bills, to college, to moral support. I was happy for them, but I found it funny how my mom wouldn't dare help me out with anything not even financially when I was their age, but wanted some sort of award when it came to buying me clothes while she was with Jed. I still am reminded of it daily that she took me shopping at a hip store back in the day. As I should be forever in debt to her for it. Again, another reason why I hate gifts, or favors from anyone.

I was the black sheep of the family, and it was clear. My mom loved Caley and Tyler so much more that they could pretty much do no wrong. They were her pride and joy as children, because although she hated Jed for breaking her heart, they were the family she wanted with him. I don't ever remember crying about feeling this was because I just always had to click into gear. I was in constant fight or flight.

Chapter Twenty-Seven

When I started dating someone new, Dane. I met him at a bar, he knew a mutual friend of mine and they introduced us. He was the farthest thing from my type. He never worked out, he grew and sold weed, he had brown stringy hair with a receding hairline, and he smoked cigarettes. I was fascinated by his confidence, however. He was witty and had this sureness of himself. Like any guy, he treated me like a princess in the beginning, and that wore off quickly. As soon as he knew he had me, he treated me terribly. He wasn't a violent person, he didn't have a temper, but he was cruel. He hated me being blonde, he hated me wearing wedges, he hated me being the life of the party. Anytime I would make a group of people laugh he was the first to make sure I knew I wasn't funny. He didn't respect me, the man I thought was so confident was clearly highly insecure. One day my car was covered in snow after a storm, so I went outside to shovel it before having to go to work. Dane just watched me struggle from his living room window while sipping his coffee and never offered to help. I have no idea what I saw in him. Dane never wanted to have sex with me either. We were together every night and I know he wasn't cheating on me, but he just had no sexual drive whatsoever. I found myself, for the first time, trying to wear something sexy so that he would give me attention, but he could walk right passed me as if I was invisible.

I was unhappy, and he made sure I felt insecure daily. One night, Dane and I went to a BBQ with some friends. A guy walked in that I had never met before. This was a small town, and I grew up here, so I knew everyone, but this guy had just moved to town, Bruce. Bruce pulled up to the BBQ in this nice white Ford Raptor truck. He had big blue eyes, nice teeth, tattoos, big arms, and style. I had a friend that moved to Tahoe a few years prior who grew up with Bruce, and she told me he was moving to Tahoe and told me he was going to love me when he met me. I paid it no mind considering I was in a relationship with Dane. But when I saw Bruce, I was all smiles. Bruce knew I was there with Dane, but he didn't care, he caught me when no one was looking and gave me his number. I was so giddy, and so sick of my sexless relationship with Dane.

About two days had passed and I still couldn't bring myself to text him. I had gotten off a long shift at the Dermatology office I worked at. I was hired and trained as a medical assistant, although I wasn't a legally certified medical assistant yet, I could still legally work under the Doctor's license and be an actual Medical Assistant. I loved my job there and I was good at what I did, I'm a fast learner and it was birth by fire there. It was busy ten- twelve-hour days but I learned something new every day. I felt stimulated and inspired. I got off work and stopped at the store before heading to Dane's house. I parked my car and started to get out of my car when a big white truck pulled up next to me and parked as well, it was Bruce. He got out of his truck, and I said, "Hey, you need help parking that thing?" in a flirty tone. "Oh hey!" He said taken by surprise. "Didn't I give you my number?" He said, he wasted no time there. "Uh, yeah… you did. But I didn't text you because I have this boyfriend thing." I said embarrassed. "Well, you obviously didn't seem too happy with him." He added. I chuckled and said, "I'll text you…"

When I got home to Dane's house whom I practically lived with, I started to secretly text Bruce. I was giddy, nervous, and excited. Dane never wanted to be around me, I don't even know why he invited me over to his house all the time, it was like I would sit on the couch while he purposely avoided me. Yet if I wasn't at his house, he'd want me over. It was the most wanted unwanted feeling ever. Bruce took me by surprise with his texts. He complimented me, made me feel beautiful, told me I deserved better, etc. He was right, I did. I decided to end things for good with Dane, which wasn't hard to do. He would dump me every few days anyways and I would come crawling back to him. I was almost counting down the days for his next issue with me so I could leave gracefully. Dane was shocked as I packed up my car and drove away. I went back to my mom's, but I stayed so busy with work, I was out of her hair for most of the time. The tough part was that if I was going to meet up with friend's later for a drink, she would get mad if I didn't invite her. To me, it wasn't appropriate to always bring my mom with me to the bars with my friend's and I who were in our mid-twenties. Anytime I took my mom out with me, she would get drunk and start a fight with someone or me. She was never a happy drunk, she was a confrontational one.

Bruce and I were enjoying our time seeing each other. He would send me flowers to my work, take me on weekend getaways, hang out with friends at his house, and it was just so my style. It wasn't like Gio's friends where it was taking shots and watching his friends take turns boxing each other, it wasn't like Dane where everyone just smoked pot and talked about snowboarding. It was my actual group of friends who all got to know and love Bruce. My sister Caley adored him, Bruce was a big family guy and came from a really loving family who were always supportive of each other. I loved that so much about him, how his family was. Caley considered him a brother-in-law already. She had seen all the losers I had gone through and this one was a prize.

It was Christmas eve and I headed over to Bruce's house. My sister Caley was already over there with her friend, which was normal. Caley would spend the night in the spare bedroom, she was a senior in high school and Jed really liked Bruce, we would have dinner at Jed's house often, so she was always with us. I walked in the door, and everyone was smiling at me. I was confused but knew they were all up to something, I looked over to the Christmas tree that Bruce and I decorated together and there was a German Shepherd puppy sitting under the tree. She slowly walked over to me as I dropped to the ground crying. "Is it mine? Is it mine?" I cried. "Yes." Bruce said. "But if we break up, is she still mine?" I cried, everyone laughed at that moment. Bruce laughed and said, "This is your dog, Candi." I walked over to him with my new puppy in her arms and hugged him. I couldn't believe he got me a puppy, and a German Shepherd at that. He knew about my tragic sudden loss of JoJo and how much it broke me, and I had told him I could never get another dog again because I no one could ever compare to JoJo, and I couldn't bear the thought of losing another animal again. But it had been over three years since losing her, so maybe this is what my heart needed.

I named my new puppy Cora Jo. I wanted her name to start with a "C" like mine, and the name "Cora" meant daughter of Zeus. I loved it, and I wanted to carry piece of JoJo within that. Cora Jo it was, she was a good girl, she was so sweet and instantly glued to me. It was crazy her bond with me right away was so similar to mine and JoJo's bond. I always felt like she was JoJo reincarnated. Cora had a great setup at Bruce's house, he was able to stay home with her during the day while I worked, and he had a job where he plowed snow in the winter, so he only had to work if there was a storm. He made a decent salary, and he came from money. He was a trust fund baby, he has never experienced financial struggle in his life, he was never actually out of money because there was a whole bank on the East coast with a pile of money in his name. I would spend every night with Bruce because now my dog was there. I couldn't take her to my mom's house, it wasn't her responsibility, and no one could watch her throughout the day as I worked such long hours.

My mom was never happy for me when it came to me dating Bruce. He was kind, he had a job, a nice truck, his own house, and he made me happy. She never truly loved that for me. I found myself trying to convince her of how great he was, but it never worked. She wasn't nice to him at first, she liked Dane and that was bizarre because he was awful to me. I came home one day to see her and said, "Did you hear Bruce got me a puppy?" I said with excitement, in hopes she would think it was sweet considering she knew how much it broke my heart to lose JoJo. "Yeah, I saw." She said in an annoyed tone. "Well, isn't that sweet?" I asked, genuinely wondering. "He should've fucking asked me first." She snapped. "What? Why would he ask you?" I replied. "Cause you fucking live with me, it's disrespectful to me thinking I want a fucking dog here." She said. I hadn't stayed at her house in months, so she wasn't making complete sense when I replied, "Well she is my dog, but she lives with Bruce and she has a good setup there, so you don't ever have to worry about her being here at your house, that's not what we were expecting." "Whatever!" She shot back while slamming a spoon down on her counter. My mom always had a temper, she would slam doors, drawers, items, you name it. I always felt like she was acting like a child. She did things like this because she knew how I usually try anything and everything to resolve an issue with her, so if she wasn't getting me begging and pleading for mercy, she would be extra loud and irritated.

Bruce's house was my safe place, he loved me, and I started to picture a future with him. Bruce and I would talk about getting married, but I always told him I didn't want kids. He was such a family man, so that bothered him. He wanted kids and to carry on his name and I cringed at the thought. I loved his family, and their dynamic, but mine wasn't like that. I just didn't see it for myself, I didn't want it for myself. As our relationship progressed, we would have our fights but never any deal breaking issues. There was a time I got wildly insecure over something he didn't even do, and I acted like a fool. I threw a fit like my mother. I think it was me testing him to see how much he really didn't want to lose me, and it was immature. I apologized the next day to him and vowed to myself to never act like that again. I felt so ashamed, I felt like my mother. I refused to ever behave like that again. Why would I be so dramatic and stupid over something that I genuinely don't want to lose? One thing about myself, is I have always been accountable. If I mess up, I will own it. I have never been raised like this clearly and that's why I take even bigger pride in owning my shit. No matter how bad it may make me look, be accountable and don't lie.

As time passed, I got a job offer at our local hospital. This was an opportunity that I couldn't pass up. This was a full-time position as a medical receptionist with benefits. They even offered a Medical Assisting program where I could finally become a Nationally Certified Medical Assistant. I was so excited, the dermatology office was sad to see me go, I gave them fair notice, and they tried to offer me a raise to keep me. I was flattered but declined, I left on good terms. I was grateful for all the experience I had there, but I needed insurance and wanted to pursue my goal to finally be an NCMA. With this certification you can go anywhere with it. And the hospital only offered it to current employees. It was an opportunity I couldn't pass up. I was in a good relationship that I wanted to grow with, and within that meant my career too.

I loved everything about the medical field. It's an ongoing study, everything is different, and there is always a high demand for it. My plan was to get into nursing school after being a Medical Assistant for a while. I wanted to learn as much as possible and work my way up. The only thing is that my mom worked for the hospital before and left on bad terms. I didn't want anyone to think I was anything remotely like her. I got this job on my own, for being me, the manager reached out to me privately because she remembered how bubbly and out-going I was when I worked as a hostess in high-school. She had told me she has always wanted to steal me for her clinic. It was a big compliment, and I felt honored. I was excited for this new chapter.

Chapter Twenty-Eight

It was summertime and Bruce had invited his family to fly in and visit us. I was so excited to meet them for the first time. My mom had eventually warmed up to Bruce and it was nice because we had planned to get our families together to go on a hike at Emerald Bay, this beautiful spot where it overlooks the lake. Tourists go there all the time for the view. Bruce had asked someone to take a picture of him and I with the beautiful background when suddenly, he got down on one knee. "Candi, I love you, will you marry me?" he said nervously while holding a beautiful ring. I didn't even know he was looking for rings! And this was really a ring I would pick myself. "Oh my god, Oh my god, yes!" I cried covering my mouth. We hugged and cried. Bruce's mom then said, "That ring was his grandmother's engagement ring." "That means you have to give it back!" My mom shouted. I was so angry my mom said that. I loved that this was a sentimental diamond, but why would my mom make it as if it wasn't mine? Why would I expect anything else from her though?

Months went on as we were happily engaged and starting to look at venues for our wedding. It was so fun trying to plan everything at first. Bruce really wanted kids, so I went to my doctor and told her that for the first time, I want to get off my birth control and start tracking my period. I had never had an actual pregnancy scare because I knew I was the only one I could trust to prevent that. I took my pill at the same time every single day. I am a very overly organized person, I am very routine, so this wasn't a chore for me, I never screwed it up. I had been on birth control for over ten years, so I was worried if maybe I couldn't even get pregnant. My doctor had me download an app where I could track my period and where I could know when I was ovulating. I wanted to be safe, but birth control free for when after we got married. I wasn't set on becoming a mom, but I was open to it if it happened.

Bruce and I went to take our engagement photos at this gorgeous meadow. I had told him he couldn't have sex with me that day because there was a ten out of ten chance I could get pregnant this day. Oh, that lit a fire inside him. He was instantly excited about it, and I went with it, I felt like there could be no way I could get pregnant this fast after only being off the pill for only a week after ten full years of it. Only about two weeks had gone by when I woke up slightly nauseous. I was at work one day when I said out loud to my co-worker,

"I think I need to take a pregnancy test." My co-worker said, "How late are you?" "I'm not late yet, but I know my body and I know my period isn't on it's way." I said jokingly yet serious. I took a test, and it was positive, instantly. I cried so hard, my wedding plans had taken a turn, my body was about to change, I didn't even know if I wanted to be a mom. I was spinning with all the thoughts in my head. One thing I knew, I wanted to be with Bruce, he was right for me, so I wasn't going to get an abortion. Why would I do that when I was with the person I am supposed to be with? Here I was planning a life with this man, and now we were pregnant, I couldn't forgive myself for terminating something that I made with the right person.

I came home and I was in tears, I ran through the front door and sat on a chair and started crying. Bruce ran up to me and said, "What's wrong? Are you hurt?" "No." I said with my face in my hands. "Did you fall on the ice?" He asked, "No." I cried out. "Are you pregnant?" He asked, "Yes." I shook my head yes with tears flowing from my face. "Yay!" Bruce said. He was excited. I wasn't devasted, I was just scared. I was scared about my body changing physically, and I didn't want to be a bad mom. I called my sister, and she told my mom, she reached out to me and said, "It's going to be okay." I needed that. I needed that support from her. My pregnancy brought Bruce and I even closer. Early in my pregnancy I started having dreams about a little blonde-haired, blue-eyed boy with an angelic face. I instantly became attached to the thought of it being a boy. We were impatiently waiting for our eleven-week checkup where we would find out the sex of the baby. I had never pictured myself to be a mom prior to getting pregnant, I never had a vision in my head, but now that I was pregnant and having these dreams, I was dead set on him being a boy. He better he a boy, I'm athletic and I was going to selfishly be devasted if it was a girl. I know people in this world wish they could only be so lucky to get pregnant period, but this was so new for me. I hadn't explored this thought process before, and it was all happening so suddenly, so I latched on to the first thing to look forward to, which was having a son.

I went and picked up the results of the genetic blood test and waited to open it with Bruce. I had my best friend Becky come over with her husband as I opened the envelope. "It's a boy!" I shouted! We all cheered; Bruce kissed me. We were so happy. I instantly knew the name I wanted for him, and I wanted Bruce's approval as well. "Babe, my name starts with a 'C' and so does Cora's. We are the girls of the house, so I was thinking that we name our son with a 'B' as well to take after you as all the boys in the house." I proposed. He loved it. We agreed on the name "Bentley." We loved it. It was a strong name, just like his dad's, and would sound good on speaker over the baseball field.

Overall, I had a very healthy pregnancy. I worked out and stayed active in a healthy way the whole time. Not to mention, I was officially in Medical Assisting program during my entire pregnancy. I worked fulltime, pregnant, and was in school five days a week. I was exhausted. Bruce and I chose to postpone the wedding. I didn't want to be pregnant on my wedding day, I wanted to be able to enjoy my night and feel beautiful. Being pregnant did not make me feel beautiful. We were fine with waiting.

Bruce and I moved into a new house together when I was eight months pregnant. I had a family friend who wanted to rent his house out and we agreed to rent it and fix it up. Our plan was to rent it, then eventually buy it, so we had no problem as tenant's putting work into it. And the owner was fine with us painting it whatever color we wanted. Moving at eight months pregnant was miserable but I was a warrior considering I moved my entire family's house out practically by myself. Being pregnant was great because I had my brother, and Bruce's friends to help. We made Bentley's future room adorable. I had picked out a cute color scheme online and Bruce and Jed were able to duplicate that. Jed helped us with almost all the projects to get the house ready and baby safe for us. Although Jed wasn't legally my stepdad, he was still my dad in my eyes. He raised me, and I respected him. We had our moments when I was younger, but I had no hostility. I never even thought about how violent he was to me when I was younger, my heart just forgave, and for him to be such a presence in my life later, when he didn't need to be, meant the world. I had zero PTSD from it, everything stemmed from my mom.

Bruce and I had discussed our birthing plan. I had told him I just wanted it to be the two of us in the delivery room. My mom increased my anxiety, and I did not want or need that. I was nervous and scared to have a baby. I was nervous to tell her what my plan was.

She was at my house visiting one day when I said, "Mom, I want to talk to you about my plan for delivery. I really just want it to be Bruce and I, the less people the better because I am nervous about all of it." I looked at her scared of her reaction when she took me by surprise and said, "I think it should absolutely just be you and Bruce." My jaw probably hit the floor at that moment. She was so cool about it, so mellow. Wow, being pregnant is a life saver I felt. "Mom, when it happens, can I ask you to come let my dog out while we are in the hospital?" I asked. "Yeah, I can do that." She replied. She made it seem like no big deal. I wanted it to be her because Cora knew her, but if she declined, we could easily ask someone else to help us out.

My due date was approaching, and I was praying little Bentley wouldn't come early. I had my final proctored exam scheduled for my Medical Assisting certification. They only did these a few times a year. I was about thirty-eight weeks pregnant and praying hard. I studied so hard and wanted this so badly. It was the day of my exam, I waddled into the testing site and checked in with this strict tall woman, built like a linebacker who was proctoring the exam. I started my test and really tried to focus on each question without rushing. You weren't allowed to go to the restroom during the exam, which was extremely difficult for a large almost full-term pregnant woman. I held my bladder, and Bentley was moving like crazy. He was an active little boy, as I held my hand on my belly just comforting his little kicks and twirls, I continued to focus on the questions. I answered my last test question when I hit submit. My results generated instantly. I passed! I was officially a Nationally Certified Medical Assistant! I have never been so proud of myself. I could do sports, and anything when it came to athletics. But something that had to do with school and studying, I struggled. I did it, and I did it pregnant, and on all on my own.

Chapter Twenty-Nine

I was officially at my due date, July 18th, pregnant, uncomfortable, and ready to be done. Bentley was moving, but not ready to come out. My OBGYN had scheduled me for an appointment the day after to discuss the next steps and get me scheduled for an induction. The morning of my appointment, I was sitting on the couch when I felt a small trickle of fluid come out. It wasn't much, but it was different. I called Bruce and let him know what had happened, and that I might need to check in to Labor and Delivery. Bruce was working for a landscaping company at the time, so he rushed home to take me to the hospital. I waddled into labor and delivery and told them what happened. "I had some fluid come out, but I know it was different." They did a swab on me, and it turns a blue color if it's amniotic fluid, it didn't turn blue. The nurse looked at me and said, "Maybe you just peed." I was so annoyed and said, "I know I'm super pregnant, and huge, but I know my holes. And I didn't pee." They advised me to keep my appointment later that afternoon with my OB. "Thank you captain obvious." I thought to myself.

Bruce and I went and got lunch about an hour before my appointment with my OB. I felt discouraged and annoyed because I knew what I felt that morning was so different. And I was scared about scheduling an induction. I had just finished my food when I felt a sudden burst of fluid rush out of me. My water broke, without question, in the restaurant. We rushed to my OB's office, and I said, "I know I'm early, but my water just broke and I'm leaking everywhere." "You need to go across the street to labor and delivery right now!" said the receptionist. "I did earlier, and they didn't believe me!" I replied. "Go now." The receptionist laughed. I worked for the hospital, so I knew everyone, and we were able to be sarcastic to each other, although I was kind of serious at this time.

We walked back into labor and delivery and the nurse that I saw earlier that morning said, "Oh I was wondering if maybe we got a false negative swab on you today…" Me, with fluid leaking down to my ankles said, "You think?" I laughed it off. One thing about me, no matter how stressed or unhappy I could be in a situation, I just couldn't bring myself to complain, or be rude to people. I had worked in many different industries, and I understood how shitty people could be when you're just trying to do your job.

As I got situated and got my epidural, Bruce had notified our family members that I was in labor. My mom came to the hospital, I had assumed to just say hi. She put her purse down and started walking around calling and texting other people. It was getting a little late when Bruce had asked her if she was going to stop by our house anytime soon. "And miss the birth of my grandson, you're tripping." She snapped. "Mom, but I need you to let Cora out." I said, timidly on the hospital bed. The nurse walked in because Bentley's heart rate started to elevate. The nurse had mentioned that he might be positioned in a certain way, which made me worry. The nurse said she would check back later and see if anything changes. "That's what happened with Tyler." My mom said to me. My mom had a very dangerous delivery when she had Tyler; he ended up being an emergency C-section and the cord was wrapped around his neck twice and he came out blue. He almost died. Why would she say that? Why would she put that in my head right now. I started to panic and couldn't relax because I pictured my newborn baby struggling and gasping for air with a cord wrapped around his neck. My mom left the hospital with attitude.

I scrolled on Facebook as I was waiting for Bentley to make his arrival. I was stressed about what my mom put in my head and stressed about my mom now being mad at me. I saw on Facebook that my mom had posted a picture of Cora and said, "Well, my daughter is in labor, and I apparently am only good for letting the dog out." I couldn't believe she was making this about her right now. I am in labor, nervous, and scared, and my mom was acting like it was poor Tinsley. She always managed to do this. For some reason I had a hard time just letting things go when it came to her. I would be overly sensitive because my mom wasn't the type to just have a disagreement and move on, I always had to be the one to say sorry, even if she was in the wrong. I always had my tail in between my legs and in way, I enabled her by doing so. I had PTSD about us not speaking for a year, and the fact that she did that so easily made me scared she wouldn't be afraid to do it again. She was just a dirty fighter; she wasn't a peaceful person to have a disagreement with, she would make sure I was punished.

It was time to push, Bentley was ready to come into this world. I pushed, and pushed and wasn't going to give up. I kept asking if they needed me to push again because I had such endurance and motivation, I was ready to do whatever the doctor told me to do. When Bentley finally came out, they immediately put him in my arms. I have never felt anything more beautiful and powerful in my life. "I'm your mommy!" I said, crying with tears of joy. That's all I could say, I was his mommy, I was going to be his mommy forever and love and protect him for the rest of my life. I was never taught this kind of love, I had never felt this kind of love, but something in me just naturally clicked when my son was placed in my arms that day. I have never seen anything more beautiful in my life. This was a love I didn't know I needed. Going from never wanting kids or family, to literally crying every day about how in love I am now with this baby I brought into this world.

Bentley was a blessing to us all, especially my family. It was as if we were brought together again through love. My mom was an amazing grandma to Bentley. She loved him dearly and it showed, I couldn't be happier that she was such a great grandma to him. Bruce and I's relationship started to shift a bit, however. It went from all this excitement and anticipation to this grand finale, to then distance between him and I. I was on maternity leave and struggling to nurse Bentley. I wasn't producing enough milk and got a bilateral breast infection which made feeding the most excruciating pain. I also tore terribly during labor, it was the worst kind of tear because I tore upwards instead of down, so I was recovering from that. I understood that as new parents we were both tired but after a few months when it was time for me to go back to work it was a struggle. I didn't mind going back to work, I loved working and missed human interaction, but I was working fulltime in a busy urgent care, pumping milk every three hours in the X-ray room, then coming home to my new baby as we were learning together. I was also trying to work out to get my body back, so I would wake up at 5am and go workout and be home before Bruce and Bentley were awake.

Bruce started to do this tit for tat thing. He would tell me that since I worked out for an hour that morning, he should be able to go golfing all day. I never told him he couldn't golf or do anything, but the way he would present it to me was extremely competitive. It didn't understand why he had to throw me trying to get my body back after being pregnant for nine months, and now lactating like a cow into being some sort of favor he was doing for me. My whole life my mom's love was only conditional, and she constantly held things over my head as collateral. I resented this kind of mentality. Bruce started his own company, a landscaping and snow removal business. He was making decent money and he came from money. But my bills weren't paid by any means, not that I expected that, but I was struggling and had paid for my medical assisting school myself, so I didn't have any financial cushion. I lived paycheck to paycheck, Bruce paid the rent, and I paid all utilities, and cable, etc. My paychecks were smaller now that I had added Bentley on my insurance. I was stressed about money, while Bruce wasn't. I won't deny that there were times if I was overdrawn, he would help me out, but I didn't see his money as my money and I hated asking for favors.

Bruce and I were rarely intimate. It's something that always bothered me because intimacy is extremely important in my eyes. It wasn't the fact that we were new parents and both tired, we were never totally sexual, but this was just another added layer to us growing apart. Planning a wedding was beyond stressful, we went from him having a trust fund that he could ask his financial advisor for money for anything, a new snowmobile, expensive equipment and machinery to start his own company, to not them being able to help much with our wedding, allegedly. We paid for majority of the wedding ourselves. I had to take a loan out of my retirement account which charges me interest on top of it. I was a little confused that his trust fund could pop out money like a vending machine whenever he wanted a new shiny toy, but for our wedding it wasn't possible. I didn't want or need an extravagant wedding, but I did want some sort of celebration. My dad didn't have money, my mom certainly didn't have money, I was on my own for this one. Bruce's parents were kind enough to buy my wedding dress which was the sweetest gesture anyone has ever done for me. But if I could do it all over again, I would've done it in a courthouse.

I found a venue that worked within our budget. It seemed perfect, it was simple, and nothing fancy. Bruce and I fought and fought leading up to the wedding and almost called it off twice. It was clear I was his opponent; we weren't a team. On our wedding day, I wasn't even excited to walk down the aisle. I was in tears, and had emotions, but I didn't walk down the aisle looking at this man as if he was the man of my dreams. He was the father of my child and loved our son dearly. But he and I didn't have a relationship between the two of us. It was like we were roommates. Our wedding was fun, our friend's and family had a great time. It was the first time my mom was going to see my dad after twenty-six years. My dad's wife Sherry was there too, and they had fun. There wasn't any bad blood between them which I loved. My dad is super easy going, can get along with anybody, and just likes to have a good time and talk about football. I get my life of the party personality from him. He could make impressions of anyone, and I could do that same. We were both complete entertainers. I loved that my mom was able to be in the same room as him and there wasn't any drama. My mom however made it a big issue that Jed was invited. She threatened not to come to my wedding which broke my heart. I eventually talked to my uncle Mark, which was her brother, and he was able to talk some sense into her about being okay with Jed being there. If I wasn't aiming to please my mom, I would've had Jed and my dad walk me down the aisle. I still regret not go forward with doing that.

I found out the day after Bruce and I got married that he had told his best friend Jeremy that if Bruce and I got a divorce he would sell his company to his friend for a cheap rate and then buy it back after our divorce. I was really offended by this, and I never said anything to him. I just let it eat me alive. This solidified that he saw me as his opponent and not a teammate.

## Chapter Thirty

Bruce and I were getting worse and worse as a couple. I won't get into the details of how bad things were getting out of respect for my son. But one-night things got bad, and I was done. I was completely done and didn't want to be with him anymore. My mom and I decided to go to the store together to get some winter clothes for Bentley, I sat in her car, shut the door and looked forward with tears in my eye. "Mom, I don't know when, but I WILL be getting a divorce one day." I couldn't even look at her when I said it because I was so numb and didn't want sympathy. I didn't want to discuss anything further, I just needed to say it.

I asked Bruce if we was willing to go to couple's counseling. I set up the appointments through my insurance and we started our sessions. Our therapist gave us some homework to do at home. She suggested that when we come home from work, that we set our phones down and tell each other three things we love about each other. I loved this suggestion because we honestly never even had conversations anymore. The next day I came home from work. I walked in the door and smiled, I set my phone down and sat next to him on the couch facing him with a big smile on my face, "Let's do our homework babe." I said with excitement. I was genuinely excited; I was hoping he would be too because it seemed like a step in the right direction. "I don't need to do this right now." He said in an annoyed toned. "What?" I said, genuinely wondering if he was serious. "This is what our therapist suggested... I'm trying here." I added. "I don't want to do it. It's stupid" he said, while he continued to scroll through his phone. I got up and walked over to tend to Bentley and went to give him a bath. I was done being sad over my marriage, I was just shut off now. I wanted to fix things, but I couldn't do it alone.

I wasn't sleeping. I would watch the clock all night and listen to meditation tape after meditation tape. I had full blown insomnia and couldn't relax. My stress kept me up all night, I couldn't shut my brain off. I was also taking college classes for my prerequisite for nursing school. We tried a total of three different marriage counselors when our final one finally set back in her chair and said, "It is good you two are separating." That hit me hard, Bruce stormed out in the middle of the session because she wasn't taking his side. Bruce was not used to not getting what he wants, his whole life he has always gotten what he wants, so the fact that this therapist was sitting here telling him he was in the wrong as we laid out all our issues, really triggered him.

I started to hangout with my friends more. My marriage consisted of me being a mommy, and then doing everything with Bruce and his friends and their wives. I was starting to just separate myself from his friends because I didn't want to be around them. It felt nice to get my groove back, I started to feel confident again because I had felt so unattractive in my marriage. The lack of chemistry, the lack of intimacy, the lack of conversation, all of it. Bruce and I continued to threaten divorce but never really pulled the plug. There was simply no way I could afford to stay in the house we were in by myself or move out. I made $21.50 an hour and paid all my own bills, including now Bentley and Bruce's full insurance benefits. My paychecks were even smaller. I couldn't focus, I wasn't sleeping and I went from having the highest grades in my college classes, to failing.

It was my thirtieth Birthday and I told Bruce all I wanted to do is go to my mom's and have dinner with her. She had moved about an hour away to Reno, NV by this time and I just wanted a night away. I didn't even plan anything with my friends, there was no point because I had given up alcohol for lent and my birthday was right in the middle of lent. I wanted a mellow birthday because I was going through so much mentally, thinking about how I am going to survive this divorce. Being a single mom with barely any income. I had started listening to this book called, "The universe has your back" by Gabrielle Bernstein. I had never turned to listening to a book before, but I was desperate for some guidance. On my drive down to my moms, I was listening to my book and heavily thinking about getting a divorce. I was sad and scared and didn't know what to do. There was a part in the book where it said to pick something that you would consider a sign. Whether it be a number, an animal, a symbol, anything, and once you see it, that is a sign that you will know you are heading in the right direction. I kept thinking about what my sign could possibly be, I have never been open to this type of thinking before, but I needed something to give me hope. "I am going to choose an owl." I said out loud to myself with a smile while gripping the steering wheel. I have never seen an owl in person before and I think they are magnificent. I continued to listen to my book and pray to God to help me bc okay during this process I was about to go through with.

I got to my mom's apartment, and we were about to get ready for dinner when she said she was going to let her dog out to go to the bathroom really quickly before she got ready. My mom put her dog on the leash and went outside. I was in my mom's bathroom putting on some mascara when suddenly, I heard "Ohooo, ooooh, ooooh." It sounded like an owl. My heart was pounding, the sound continued and sounded really close. I slowly walked over to a window in my mom's bedroom and opened the blinds, a big brown owl with big yellow eyes was sitting on a post right outside the window. He slowly turned his head and looked right at me. We made complete eye contact for about five seconds before he flew away. I had chills, this was my sign, my confirmation from the Universe, from God, that I was going to be okay with the direction I was going.

I started to feel a little more comfort with my decision. When I got back home the tension was at an all-time high between us. I started to become so disconnected and so did he. I just knew that no matter what, I refused to let my son grow up in a household where there was fighting, arguing, and lacked love between his mommy and daddy. I'd rather being alone then to be unhappy with someone. I would hang out with my friends and vent to them about what was really going on. I stopped posting pictures of Bruce and I and instead posted pictures of Cora, Bentley, and myself. I started to gain this confidence and security within myself knowing that I deserved better which in turn made Bruce's friends started a rumor that I was having an affair. Bruce would have his friend Jeremy stalk me when I went to hang out with my girlfriend's. He would take pictures of where my car was and was not. Bruce's other friends were helping to assist him in this at times. I felt suffocated, I felt like there was no escape. As Bruce and I discussed separation/ divorce I told him I couldn't afford to live anywhere in Tahoe with my income. He made it clear he wouldn't help me financially and I didn't expect him to, but I had to move in with my mom. I told him right off the bat that I wouldn't take full custody of Bentley because although we had our differences, he was a great dad. I told him I will agree to fifty-fifty custody right away. I would have Bentley with me on my days, and I chose to commute, for work and for Bentley's daycare. I chose not to uproot Bentley's life entirely, so I kept him in the current Daycare he was enrolled in because he was only three and comfortable at this daycare and I was comfortable with them as well. It's a lot of stress to find a Daycare that you trust and that has vacancy, I couldn't bear the thought of my son having to go to a brand-new place that he wasn't familiar with on top of him and his mommy sleeping at a new place every night. I chose to move; therefore, I chose to keep everything as stable for Bentley as possible.

Moving into my mom's two-bedroom apartment was hard considering Tyler lived with her so he had a bedroom, and I shared a bed at the age of thirty, with my mom. I got Bentley a toddler bed next to me. I couldn't take Cora with me right away because I worked such long hours and had a commute, I couldn't leave her in an apartment on the second floor all day. I didn't want to do that to her either. I would take her on weekends and bring her back until I could hopefully get on my own two feet and find a place where I could have her. As Bruce and I talked further about filing for divorce, we finally did it. We decided to keep the lawyers out of it since we agreed on sharing custody, and I told him I wouldn't ask for child support or alimony. I would rather live broke and have zero drama with Bruce than to fight for financial help where he would make my life hell. I went to the courthouse to sit with the court appointed mediator to sign my share of the papers. She didn't represent either of us, it was just simply to make sure everything was correct in our papers and properly signed. She went over my income, and my bills and saw that I was making hardly any money. She asked me about my engagement ring, Bruce took it. He took it out of my drawer and refused to return it. When I asked for it, he said "It's my Grandma's." I didn't even want the ring, but that comment confirmed that everything was conditional, even his proposal. The representative at the court put her glasses down and rubbed her eyes as if she was preparing to say something big, "You really aren't going to go after him for child support? And ask for the ring back? It's legally yours." She spoke. "I just don't want any drama." I said sadly as I looked down. I was praying that if I chose not to go after him for what was legally mine, then he would be civil. He threatened to ruin my life if I did, but I chose not to tell her that because I didn't want more attention to this. She looked disappointed,

"I'm not even representing you, and I really think you need to rethink this Candi, you are getting burned here, and I'm not even allowed to tell you that." She added. "I'm okay." I replied hesitantly.

I was struggling, really struggling. I was constantly overdrawn in my account, sleeping next to my mom, and hated that my son wasn't with his mommy every night. I called Bruce and said, "Can you please help me with a little bit of money Bruce? I am really struggling right now." I was fighting back tears and my voice was cracking. "I'm not paying you shit Candi, you should've never left. This is the consequence." He said. "Bruce, I can't even afford chicken nuggets! Can you please just like get me a gift card to the grocery store?" I pleaded. "Nope." He said. He loved that I was struggling, he needed to be in power. "Bruce, I could've gotten over $4,500 from you per month if I went forward with child support, and I didn't. All I am asking is for a little help with food? My mom can't pay for all our food, and I am driving more and spending any extra cash on gas." I pointed out. "You wouldn't get shit from me for child support." He fired back. He was wrong, the difference in our income was more than double. I made close nothing, plus I was still paying for his full benefits. I couldn't kick him off my insurance until we were legally divorced. "I'm struggling Bruce, badly." I cried. "You can come back then. You wouldn't have to worry about anything if you just came back." He said. I was so offended, he didn't even care that I could barely afford to feed our son, and then wanted me to come crawling back if I wanted financial stability. I didn't want financial stability, I wanted love. I just wanted to be in love, madly in love. I would rather be poor then to come back to a relationship that wasn't good for me or my son.

A good mom is a happy mom. I stand by that. When I was married, I was so unhappy, my energy was robbed constantly, and I felt like I wasn't a truly happy person which robbed my energy when I was with my son. Being at my mom's wasn't a positive thing, but I was happier in general, therefore I felt like a more attentive and loving mom. My son was my world, and being the best mother could be for him was all that mattered.

Chapter Thirty- One

It was 2020, the pandemic had hit, and the world was a depressed pile of unknown shit. This also meant that this was going to delay the finalization of our divorce. We were signed on both parts and the papers were literally sitting on a judge's desk collecting dust. As much as I wanted it to be over and done with, I didn't care. I wasn't going to let a piece of unsigned paper dictate if I could move on or not. I did what every newly single person does and downloaded dating apps. I was so picky and was not going to settle for just anyone. I wasn't interested in ever being in a relationship again to be honest, I just wanted some good conversation with a male for once.

My mom was still her same old self, she would drink and then pick a fight. I couldn't escape it because she was letting me live with her. She would cuss me out, slam things around, and all in front of Bentley. I am a very clean person so I would make sure I always kept her apartment spotless, I did her laundry, organized her closet, I did anything I could to help keep her satisfied. One night I had asked her not to give Bentley some juice when she flipped out on me. She was tipsy and continued to call me a "Helicopter mom." She kept repeating it over and over and over all in attempt to hurt my feelings. I knew I wasn't a "Helicopter mom," but it was the mere fact that she was putting so much energy into trying to offend me. Bentley was with me that night and I laid with him and just held him in his bed. I needed to get out of this situation.

I started to work overtime and was lucky enough to work in healthcare, so I was an "essential worker." I was driving to work one morning hating my life, hating my situation. "How can I live like this? How can I always be this poor? Please God, please God I need something. I need something." I cried this out loud as I was squeezing my steering wheel. I was begging for a miracle. A week later I got my tax return, and it was enough to pay for a deposit to rent an apartment. I was so ready to move out. It was a cute, one-bedroom apartment that Bentley and I could call home. I was able to move in quickly and felt so good about it. For once, my own place, my own space. Bentley and I will have a safe, peaceful home together. It had a pool where I would take him swimming, and I signed him up for a gymnastics place right around the corner. We loved it.

I had started to post on this app called "Tik Tok" my sister had told me about. Everyone talked about it, and I had no idea what I was doing on there. One day I decided to post a funny video of me dancing to a remix of a kid's song. I always had rhythm, I was a pretty good dancer and was voted "Best to dance with" in high school. I posted the video and moved on about my week. I was doing the dishes at my mom's place when my sister called me. "Sis, you're literally viral." She said. "What? I didn't post anything on Instagram." I said, highly confused. "No, Tiktok... you're huge on there." She replied. "What? I didn't even think I knew what I was doing on there? I haven't even been on the app in two weeks, I forgot about it." I said. I went and looked, and my video had millions and millions of views, I grew this TikTok following overnight, which grew my Instagram following overnight. This was birth by fire in a sense because I was eaten alive by people who were now obsessed with me and obsessed with hating me. I started to feel this pressure to keep up with content and it became a regular thing. I loved making impressions and entertaining, so I treated this like it was an acting gig, and at times I would share my opinions on divorce with added comedy. People really started to relate to that. I became this image of what single moms can really overcome, and that there is such thing as happiness after divorce. I loved being this inspiring image for women all around the world. Women would reach out to me daily thanking me for showing them it's okay to defend yourself and to be confident. It felt so good to be such a role model for women who needed it most. Throughout life, I couldn't stand the thought of knowing someone was insecure, I would always go out of my way to compliment people. Knowing if someone felt uncomfortable made me feel uncomfortable. Some people would easily say this is a beautiful characteristic, but it is also something that triggered me deep inside. It was always as if I made it my duty to make others feel better because as I grew up, if my mom was in a mood or seemingly unhappy, I would get this extreme anxiety because I knew I had to make her feel better or I'd pay for it. She would make sure that if I didn't cater to her emotions, that I would be punished in some way.

As the world was slowly allowing businesses to open back up here and there, I had gone on a few dates. I honestly went out with some really great guys. I had a good gauge right off the bat of what I would and wouldn't deal with. I had never felt more beautiful and sexier in my life. I was at this place in my life where I knew exactly what I wanted, love and respect. I had the marriage, I had the child, I had the wedding, I had the white picket fence, I wasn't looking for that ever again, I wasn't in need of that. I had my son, and he was my world, and I wasn't looking to have more, I never wanted to get married again. It felt good to go on a date knowing I didn't have this fantasy of some American Dream anymore. I just felt so sure of myself, and ever so confident. I wasn't going to let anyone meet my son unless it was a serious relationship, for which I wasn't dying to look for. I was pretty emotionally unavailable you could say. I wanted to fall in love one day but wasn't losing sleep over it by any means. I almost acted like a dude, I would ghost guys, I would be hard to get ahold of, I didn't care to be consistent, I didn't commit to anyone. I would date on the days I didn't have Bentley, and when I had him, it was mommy and son time only. I didn't think I would have it any other way considering I was happy for once.

After a while, I met someone, Nick. Nick was a firefighter. He recognized me from my work when we would have the firefighters and medics transfer patients if need be. He saw my profile on a dating app and reached out. He said he saw me at my work, then looked at my name on my badge a year ago, looked me up on Facebook and saw that I was married. He was so excited to find out I was officially single. I was flattered. He was a father of two, a son and a daughter, they were teenagers. He really pursued me in the beginning and caught my interest. Things took a turn after a couple months and this time he was the emotionally unavailable one. We dated regularly but not exclusively. He didn't want to commit to me, and I acted like I didn't care. I was never going to allow a guy to know if they affected my emotions. I dated other guys as well, I wasn't sitting at home waiting for him to call me, I stayed busy, although deep down I wanted him to always call. Nick was a partier. He liked to drink and drink a lot. I didn't think much of it considering he was a firefighter and was able to hold a good job. He was open about how much he liked to party, but always justified it considering when he was at the fire station he was obviously sober.

One day I was sitting at home scrolling on Instagram when I randomly came across my friend Ray's post. He posted a quick story of him and a friend he was with. I have never done this, but something gave me this urge to message him and ask him who it was that was with him in the photo. Ray replied and said it was his friend "Kyle." "What's his Instagram?" I quickly asked Ray. I was ready to add him. Who was I? I had never gone out of my way to reach out to a guy in my life, what had come over me? "He doesn't have social media." Said Ray. I thought that was even more attractive. I guy who didn't have social media was so hot and mature to me. A guy, who wasn't desperate to be on the internet, showing off, liking girl's photos, etc. "I showed him your profile, he thinks you're cute." Ray said to me. Ray ended up linking us up. We only started to text each other and get to know each other by phone for months. Kyle lived two hours away from me, he was five years older than me, never been married, and never had any kids. He was a police officer and didn't care to party, didn't really like to drink, and loved working out. He was so my style. We talked every single day and facetimed here and there. After about six months of talking, we finally decided to meet. I went shopping at the mall with a friend of mine and he decided to meet up with me really quickly while he was patrolling. He pulled up in his squad car and got out. He was tall, muscular, brown hair, blue eyes, and the most handsome man I have ever seen. I ran and jumped into his arms instantly. It was like out of a movie, he picked me up and held me as if I weighed nothing. He was so strong and took my breath away. We talked for a while and held hands the entire time and kissed each other goodbye. When I got home, I was smitten. But still wrapped around Nick's finger at the same time. Nick lived in my same city, and we had been seeing each other regularly so I felt a little attached. I constantly thought about Kyle though, I just didn't know where his head was at with him and I and I was too proud to make him talk about it. Kyle was always in control of his emotions, and not easily vulnerable. He was just so genuine and matter of fact, but also made it hard to read. I felt intimidated because I was divorced, had a son, and I wasn't making money. I lived paycheck to paycheck, and I felt as if he was too good for me. I have never felt that insecure about a guy, and he never made me feel that way, but it was all internal. Kyle was such a catch, and I couldn't believe that me, a girl who has been quite confident her whole like when it came to relationships, felt like I wasn't good enough. We continued to talk to daily, and I loved it.

I still chose to keep my options open and went on dates here and there. I felt like I'd be a fool to put all my eggs in one basket whether it was Kyle or Nick. I didn't want to get hurt so I was quite guarded and chose to keep myself distracted. Meanwhile, Bruce hated the fact that I was really moving on. Deep down he had hoped that we would rekindle possibly. I didn't want my marriage to fail, I wanted to be with my husband forever, this wasn't my vision for us either, but I tried, I really did try. Bruce would constantly say I didn't try hard enough, and I gave up too easily, and I disagree. Three marriage counselors later, sleepless nights, and endless communication of what was bothering me felt like I really did try. I hardly cried after my divorce because I had mourned the loss of my marriage during my divorce. All I knew is that I was grateful that we had met, and had our son, because he is the biggest blessing in the world.

## Chapter Thirty-Two

I continued to stay consistent with being open about my divorce, struggles, and emotions as a single mother on TikTok. My following was continuing to grow. One day, someone reached out to me saying that there was a website profile posing as me and alluding to selling inappropriate photos. I felt sick to my stomach and started to panic. I quickly ran to the website that was posing as me and saw that they had stolen my bikini photos from the internet and was charging money for people to gain access to more explicit pictures. I quickly e-mailed the customer support for a request to remove this account. Luckily, I was able to get this profile taken down in a timely manner. However, as my social media platform continued to grow, this continued to happen. People posing as me, trying to scam people out of money, etc. I noticed on one website where yet another fake profile was made had over two thousand subscribers. "Wow" I thought to myself. "That many people want to see a sexier side of me?" I was able to dispute that profile and thought to myself, "Well hey, they're just bikini photos. What if I make my own account, and only post bikini photos on there and charge for that?" I decided to take the risk and do it. I created an account on Only Fans. Before I knew it, I had over one thousand subscribers, paying monthly to see me. I started to do my research, I dove into any and all videos and articles on how to run a successful Only Fans page. I was always body and sexually confident, I didn't see the harm in being proud of that and monetizing it. I started to make a little more content, and slowly but surely getting a little more explicit. Money was just coming in, money that I had never even thought would be possible for me to make. This sounds crazy, but I really do thank the Universe for how this all happened. Had these people not tried to pose as me and scam others, I would have never thought to do this.

Starting this kind of account, and being from a small town, word got out quick. Bruce's friends were all subscribing to me, which felt so violating. They all loved to talk poorly about me, yet they were dying to see explicit photos of me. I was angry at first, but then I realized that I just needed to own it. I wasn't going to pretend like I wasn't running an account like this. This kind of money finally allowed me to pay my rent, buy groceries comfortably, take my son to the trampoline park. It wasn't about shopping and gifts; it was about being financially secure for the first time in my life. Word got back to Bruce about my Only Fans account, and he threatened to fight for custody. I was shaken up by this, I didn't know what to do. If I deleted it, I would go back to always being stressed, and overdrawn in my account, what was I going to do? I. consulted with an attorney and to my surprise, they reassured me that having a legal, explicit, tax paying business does not make someone lose custody. There are literally porn stars and strippers who have full custody. I felt more confident with this knowledge and chose to continue to own it and not be ashamed by it. Sure, some people would frown upon it, but they weren't in my shoes. Bruce had no right to even share his opinion with me about it because he certainly refused to help me financially. And the people from my small town didn't pay my bills either, so I continued to focus on myself, my bills, and carry on with that mindset. Many would say it's trashy, but it isn't to me. Playboy magazine was considered classy and tasteful, and this was simply an online version of that. I wasn't doing porn, and I certainly wasn't at a strip club. This sort of job really empowered me, I was the boss of myself. I chose what I wanted to post and when I would do it. And to be honest, most of the men who subscribed just wanted to have a conversation. These were genuine fans of me, people who wanted to feel a sense of closeness to me. They had to pay to see my photos and had to pay to message me. I had my own moral compass within that, no one was allowed to have my number, and no one was allowed to see me in person. I would get countless offers, sometimes over ten thousand dollars to simply go to dinner with a guy, and the answer is always no. I'm not shaming other women who do that, but to me, that is breaking my privacy and safety. I wasn't a sugar baby, or an escort. Money couldn't convince me to break my own rules I had laid down for myself. It was online pictures and conversation or nothing. I felt in total control, and I was proud of myself for how I was operating it. I was also very open to my mom about it. How could she judge me anyway, it's not like she helped me financially ever either. She was actually pretty accepting of it which meant the world to me. My biggest thing is to always remain honest in life. I own my truth, and never pretend like I was someone I wasn't. If anyone had anything negative to say about my explicit content, I wouldn't care, if I were to die and go to Heaven today, I wouldn't say, "Darn, I really regret selling those photos and having a safe place and food on the table for my son." I was always very witty and always had a comeback for everything. People could easily think I was a bitch for that, but to me, I had no tolerance for people trying to bring me down. I dealt with it my whole life; I no longer need to make myself smaller to make others happy.

My whole life I have had to defend myself, and struggle, so I wasn't going to allow people to try and hurt my feelings when they haven't walked a day in my shoes. Random people on the internet could not hurt me, and I think it is because I have had people that I actually know, and love hurt me in real life. Therefore, why would a complete stranger offend me? I have never been judgmental of people, and I would never go out of my way to hurt anyone, so it angered me that people would do it to me. It was never the words that hurt me, it was always the audacity that people had to try and go out of their way to offend someone. That's what bothered me most, I hated seeing people in this world, or online who were being teased or made fun of. It made me want to always protect the weaker man. For me, it was almost as if I preferred people to be cruel to me instead of others because I knew I could handle it. As I continued to defend myself and others online, I became known as this girl on TikTok who "Took no shit." "The Vigilante." "The Beth Dutton of TikTok." I would and increasing amount of comments and messages from women who thanked me for showing them it's okay to be confident and set boundaries. This was the most rewarding feeling in the world, showing women they are valued, they are beautiful, and that anyone who is trying to bring you down is already beneath you. In a world full of bullies, I was a Vigilante.

## Chapter Thirty-Three

My mom had decided to move out of her apartment in Reno and buy a place. She chose a modular home in a tailer park. The neighborhood seemed surprisingly quiet, but the neighbors were odd. The family that lived next door to my mom's new place had constant drunken fights, and the father of the house was always on some sort of drugs. I was so grateful that Bentley and I had moved out when we did, because I wouldn't feel comfortable with us living there. Bruce ended up buying the house we lived in; I was happy for him. My brother Tyler still lived with my mom and my sister Caley was living in Arizona. She was finishing up nursing school.

I continued with my Medical Assisting job, and my side hustle doing Only Fans. I was very honest about this with Nick as well. He didn't judge me for it, but also, he saw women as objects anyways. I never told Kyle about it however, he had such integrity, and I didn't want him to think less of me. Although I was so unapologetically me, with him I wanted to look better. If he asked, I would be honest. But I didn't feel the need to disclose any of that information considering I didn't even know how serious he was about me. I prayed and prayed however for some sort of change. I didn't want to do Only Fans forever. One day I decided to look at my direct messages on Instagram, I rarely checked them seeing as I would receive an overwhelming amount of messaged daily from my viewers. For some reason, something told me to open one specific message, it was a casting producer. This producer reached out and said, "Hi there, I am a casting producer, and we are planning on filming a new upcoming show. We have been watching your content on your platforms and think you would be perfect for this new show." I was so skeptical at first and was somewhat cold in my response as I thought it was a scam and or a human trafficker. The producer graciously encouraged me to look them up for verification. They were, in fact, a true production company. I decided to proceed to with their interview and get a little more information about it. This concept of the show was to have six previously divorced "couples" on a dating show. Where they either find new love, or rekindle with their ex. The only kicker was that Bruce would have to be on the show as well. I reached out to Bruce and told him about this opportunity for us to be on a TV show. He was excited, "I was built for reality TV!" He said. I chuckled because, he was right, he had a good personality, loved reality TV, and was full of drama.

Bruce and I went forward with the casting, interviews, and auditions. We were officially casted to be on the show. They flew us out to Costa Rica to film the show. My mom watched Bentley, Cora, and Bruce's dog while we went to film. We were able to facetime once daily during filming, and I had paid her five hundred dollars for being so kind to help. Bruce's mom would have been willing to do the same, but Bentley was closer to my mom and much more comfortable with her since Bruce's mom lived in the Midwest and hasn't been around much. I told Bruce I had paid my mom for helping us and encouraged him to do the same.

Filming the show was a wild, once in a lifetime experience. I went on the show not hoping to meet someone new, but I was hoping Bruce would. I wanted him to get his confidence back and to meet someone amazing. He was still so hard to co-parent with because he was still angry about the divorce. I felt like if he met someone, and fell in love, then we would be more civil. During the filming process, I often thought about both Kyle, and Nick. They both knew I was going on the show, but neither of them had ever seemed like they wanted to be more serious with me, so I had no hesitations about pursuing the opportunity presented to me. I was single, so I had no loyalty to anyone at that time. Although, still hoped that Nick would finally want to commit to me one day.

After filming, when I returned home, I squeezed Bentley and Cora as if it had been years. I was so happy to be home. Some time had passed as I focused on myself, and my son when I went down to visit Kyle. Kyle and I were talking more consistently, but I just felt like that's all it ever was going to be. He didn't talk to me about how he felt about me, or what he saw in me, and I didn't want to pressure him by any means. I just enjoyed our conversations and time together when we could. Nick and I were hanging out more and more as well, when finally, I told him I was talking to someone else and didn't want to be strung along any further. It had been a year of us just being hookup buddies, and nothing more and I was at the point in my life where I was sick of it and wanted something serious now finally. As soon as he heard someone else might be catching my attention, he quickly made me his girlfriend. I was flattered, but annoyed this was the reason why he committed. I went along with it when after a couple weeks, Kyle reached out and asked, "Is the reason you disappeared on me is because you have a boyfriend?" I was honest with him and told him "Yes, I have a boyfriend now, I am sorry." Kyle, being the standup man that he is said, "Well I appreciate you being honest with me, but I think it's more of a convenience thing seeing as your new dude lives closer." I said, "I am sorry." He then added, "I'm just a little confused because I thought we were heading in that direction." I was shocked, and sad. We were talking more and more; however, he had never told me that's where his head was at with me. I felt like a complete jerk and apologized. I kept thinking about how he was such a respectful man for not cussing me out. I know I probably would have if someone did that to me.

My relationship with Nick was wild. Bruce was angry I had a boyfriend, but he was angry with me regardless. Nick was always wanting to havea good time, he just wanted to drink, golf, and go to bars with me. I found myself drinking more than I personally liked to. I felt unhealthy and disappointed in myself. Not to mention, I was paying for everything. I am not sure why, but ever since I had started to make money, I was overly generous about it, with anyone. I loved to show my love by buying gifts for people or treating them to things. My mom and I went to an appointment for her to get lip injections, and I snuck out of the treatment room to use the restroom and went to the front desk to pay for her services. Even when I had no money, I always made sure I got my mom something for her birthday, or Mother's Day. Not to put my siblings down, but they wouldn't even get her anything for holidays sometimes. I just always wanted to make her feel special and hoped it would make her love or appreciate me. It was always unnoticed. Nick was so used to me paying for everything, he would send me a picture of expensive golf clubs because he knew I would run down to the golf store and get them. I paid for countless trips, vacations, and his kids. His daughter wasn't close with her mom and lacked any sort of beauty help or advice. I would pay to get her hair done, buy her makeup, anything to make her feel more confident seeing as she only lived with her dad and was a quiet, somewhat timid girl.

I would often go on a three-mile run around this beautiful neighborhood. I would jog, and just imagine how amazing it would be to live in this neighborhood, with these adorable houses, and how I could just run every day, and bring Cora with me. She was still back and forth from my house to Bruce's almost as if she would just come with Bentley when Bruce and I would exchange. I was imagining myself living in this neighborhood, and taking it all in. When I got back to my apartment, I opened my laptop just to see what the prices were like in that area. My eyes grew huge as I saw that just two hours ago, a posting for a home for rent was available in that neighborhood. I got chills, I applied immediately. I had been at my apartment for over a year now, and I wanted Bentley to be able to have a backyard, as all we had was a little dark porch, if we wanted to play baseball or soccer, we had to load up the car and go to the park. I wanted him to have his own room and a yard. The owners called me and asked me to come by the place and meet them, they loved me, and I loved them! The house was beautiful, and expensive, but I could do it. We were able to move in after a few weeks. Bentley was so excited and so was I. This was our home, it was bright, and sunny, and our neighbors had kids his age. My heart was so full, I loved that Bentley had a home like this with me, our apartment was amazing for the two of us, but he was five years old now and getting bigger. Sharing a room was getting tough, and his dad had the nice house, the huge backyard, the nice RV, the motorcycles, the snowmobiles, etc. I wanted to at least be able to play baseball with Bentley in the backyard.

I finally let Nick meet Bentley after a few months of being official. He was great with him, and I loved that. I felt like since Nick was a dad himself, it wasn't going to be weird. I felt that if this were Kyle, it might be weird to him seeing as he didn't have kids of his own and he might not like how my life is. Time went on and Nick would send me vacation destinations because he knew I would just simply book them and pay for it all. Looking back on things now, I can't believe that a man with a good paying job could just easily take money from a single mom. I loved him, so I never thought anything of it at the time. Nick would always ask me how much money I was making on Only Fans, and I would tell him, which I regret because clearly this is how he knew he would be securing his endless vacations and presents. He would text me and say things like, "Let's get rich babe." I hated it, all he talked about was getting rich, I didn't care for that. I just wanted to pay my bills and be in love. I wanted text messages that said, "I love you and want to be with you forever." Things that money can't buy.

Nick continued to drink a lot, and he started to get insecure. He would come home from golfing and drinking all day and start fights. He would get so angry about how the TV show was coming out, and how I was probably going to leave him for someone famous. That's not at all what I wanted. He grew more and more insecure as I was starting to get well known websites wanting to confirm my birthday, place of birth, and my TikTok fame as I was known as a popular search on the internet. Little did he know, I had already had famous athletes messaging me left and right just from them seeing my TikTok. I wasn't interested even in the slightest. I had my own money, my own show coming out, and I valued love and loyalty. Why would I waste my time being flattered by some athlete who would end up cheating on me anyways? No thanks, that wasn't appetizing even in the slightest. As Nick would pick these fights with me, he would have no problem yelling at me either. I had come such a long way, that I got to a point in my life where I was not going to stoop to his level. I wasn't going to yell back; I wasn't going to engage in this toxicity. He would storm out of my house, and then apologize the next day. One night, I was crying so hard on my bedroom floor about how I was sick of this relationship and being with such a mean drunk, when I got a text message. "Hey you, hope you're doing well. I miss you." It was Kyle. I don't know how, but he would manage to text me at the times I needed him most. It was like God was sending me signs left and right that this man is the man I need to be with.

One day I had Cora at my mom's house because I had to work a long shift and she had indoor/ outdoor access at my mom's. She had such bad separation anxiety and the second I dropped her off, I had an uneasy feeling that whole day. I couldn't even concentrate at work; my gut was telling me something was seriously wrong. When I rushed back home to my mom's house to get Cora, she was gone. She was not there, I dropped to my knees. She had been at my mom's for an entire day plenty of times, how did this happen? My fingers went numb, and I started to see black. Cora was my world, my everything, and she was scared to ever go up to strangers. She only really trusted me. I called Nick who was golfing and cried to him on the phone, "Cora's missing Nick!." I could barely even think straight. Nick said he'd be right there to help me. But it took him hours, he had clearly finished his game of golf. Where I was posting on every single app and making phone calls and driving around to find her. When Nick finally met with me to help me find her, he had reeked of booze. I didn't care, I just wanted my dog. I was in tears and trying hard to focus as we were driving around the neighborhood. "You need to calm down. You're freaking out." Nick said to me in the car. "What?" I said, I was genuinely confused, I was oddly calm, I almost had no energy to freak out. I couldn't even believe what he was saying, not to mention he knew how much I loved my dog. "I'm sad Nick." I said quietly. He made it seem like such an inconvenience he was helping me look for her. I was so angry with him deep down but didn't have time to deal with it because I just cared to find Cora. I got a text message from Kyle. "Hey you, I saw that your Cora was missing. Do you need my help? I will take off from work and come help you look for her." "I'm a mess right now Kyle, thank you. I will let you know." I replied while tears were pouring down. I couldn't believe that my own boyfriend was next to me making me feel like I ruined his night, while Kyle offered to drive two hours to come help me look for my dog.

Morning came and my brother Tyler walked outside of my mom's house and saw Cora in a grass patch across the street. She had wandering back and was confused, and limping. She had clearly been running scared all night. I rushed back over to my mom's to come get her. I was crying and so grateful she was home safe, I loved her so much and she loved me. Her poor paws were raw, and she was very sore. But she was home, and I thanked God for that. I was laying on the floor next to her when Nick said, "I'm glad you found her cause I was worried our Mexico trip was going to be canceled." I was speechless. Of course, he said that. I had booked and paid for a luxury resort for us in Mexico and it was just a week away, that's all he cared about. "Well, yeah. If I didn't find Cora, I wouldn't have gone to Mexico. I would be miserable Nick." I said. "Yeah I know, it was like we were either going to cancel it, or you were just going to ruin the trip by being sad the whole time." He added. What a selfish ass hole I thought. I loved him, but what the hell was I doing? Every muscle in my body knew that I was meant to be with Kyle. I missed him so much.

Chapter Thirty-Four

My friend Alyssa and her mom Theresa were in Reno and invited my mom and I out to dinner. We all caught up and they had asked me about my experience filming the show. I could tell my mom was getting annoyed that all the attention was on me. The more questions they asked the more uncomfortable I felt because I could see my mom growing even more aggravated. My mom was drinking wine, so I could see it in her eyes. She was like a ticking time bomb. She hated the fact that I had this sort of attention. "Yeah, well you could only go because I watched Bentley and the dogs for you." She snapped. "Yes mom, and I am very grateful for that." I said calmly yet triggered. "Yeah, so you better be buying me a house." She said sarcastically. This however wasn't entirely sarcastic. This was her way of saying I owe her. "Mom, some grandparents are thrilled to spend a few weeks with their grandkids. I used to go to my grandmas for weeks, and she loved it." I snipped back. My mom got louder at the table and said, "Really? Really? Your grandma didn't have a fucking full-time job and had to take care of two dogs on top of it." This is where I crumble, this is where she enjoys getting louder because she knows I will coward down because she knows how much I hate scenes. I got quiet as my mom continued with her little digs here and there the rest of dinner.

Alyssa and Theresa decided to go back to my mom's house to hang out for a bit longer and see my mom's new place. Alyssa decided to drive with me, and Theresa drove with my mom. As we pulled up to my mom's, my mom walked inside first. Theresa pulled me aside and said, "You know Candi, your mom just feels really hurt by you and that you were really ungrateful for her watching Bentley and the dogs while you were in Costa Rica." "What? Theresa, I have been more than grateful, I talked to her a Bentley every day I was there, and I did this for a potential career in the film industry. I am beyond thankful. I literally paid her five hundred dollars!" I stated. "You paid her?" Theresa asked. "Yes! I literally paid her, and so did Bruce." I reiterated. "Well, she said you didn't pay her." Theresa said, changing her tone. I think she realized she had nothing left to point out after I let her know the truth. I walked inside my mom's house heart broken. How could she lie and say that I didn't pay her? Why does she lie about me? I felt hurt, and angry. But I pretended like nothing happened so there wasn't any drama in front of Alyssa and Theresa.

A few days later I was back at my mom's house for dinner while Bentley was with his dad. My mom had some wine and was in another mood. For the longest time I just wanted to say, "I'm not coming over for dinner if you're drinking." But that would start a fight. Don't get me wrong, I love wine with dinner too, but I wasn't a confrontational drinker. My mom had made some rude comment, when I finally called her out about lying to Theresa about me not paying her to watch Bentley while I filmed the show. I told her she completely lied. She was enraged, she was infuriated that she was caught. Once again it was like watching a little kid throw a temper tantrum. She started screaming and called me every single name in the book. I for once, continued to focus on my breaths. I usually get really worked up when tremble when my mom and I fight, and this time I just kept telling myself not to react the way she wants me to. This made her more upset that I was being so mature. "You don't need to scream at me, that's not how I talk to you and that's not how I have a conversation." I said calmly. This triggered her so she decided to get the reaction she was longing for when she suddenly took her wine glass and slammed it on the counter with her hand. The glass went through the stem, and it cut her hand. I looked at it, and looked at her and said, "Wow. Get ahold of yourself." This was probably bitchy, and I didn't care. I meant it. Who acts like that when they're fifty-five years old? I hope I made her feel stupid. "Get the fuck out of my house you stupid fucking bitch." She screamed. I slowly walked out, in tears. I got in my car and cried behind my steering wheel. This was my mom. This was always going to be my mom. All I do is try, I try so hard, and she hates me. My mom hates me, she looked at me like she hated me, she constantly wanted to bring me down, she never liked anything I said or did. It hurt so much. I called Jed crying. "Candi, only you can control your reaction to it. Your mom has a lot of issues, and you can't be around her when she's drinking." He was right. I would always make a promise to myself I wouldn't be around her when she's drinking, but when she was sweet and would invite me over for dinner, I had always hoped it would be a good night together. This made me latch on to other relationships, because if I didn't have her, I had no one. There was never an "I'm sorry" from my mom, but she would text me the next day asking if I wanted to go to dinner, or if she could come over and see Bentley and bring dinner. I always said yes because I was always so desperate to keep the peace.

Meanwhile, Nick was growing more and more comfortable with these blowout fights himself. I had told him I was going to do a sober month and asked if he would do it with me. He said he would. I felt so excited because I felt like this would be good for us. He lasted four days. He was back to drinking and I stayed strong. I always do a complete sober month every year because it reminds me that I am always in control, and it is a nice, healthy reset. Nick would start and argument and I would remain calm. "Oh, you think you're all high and mighty cause you're not drinking. Sorry you're majesty." He would drunkenly say. "I never said I was high and mighty; you just think I am." I would clap back. He was angry I wasn't going to engage with an argument. I had no fight left in me after the shit my mom has put me through. I just got sick of it. I would rather be alone than to have a relationship where I was screaming and fighting ever again. Nick always made sure he never pulled these drunken fights on front of Bentley which was good. But still, he was hardly ever sober in general. I realized I didn't want this as my boyfriend, or as Bentley's stepdad. I started to realize I deserved so much better and that I was being taken advantage of. I started spoil him less and less. He noticed this shift in my behavior. His daughter said she was hungry one night and wanted Mexican food for dinner. I wasn't hungry, but normally I would just pick up my phone and order something and pay for everyone. This time, I stayed strong. "Nick, she wants Mexican food. Do you want to order that?" I asked. "Wow." He replied. "What? She's hungry." I pointed out. "Do you want to order that?" He mocked me in this added smirky tone. "What's wrong? She is hungry, I am not." I stated. He was livid as he ordered her food, he didn't speak to me the rest of the night. He sipped his beer and avoided me at all costs. If I did ask him something, he was short with his reply. I hated this tension; I wasn't the type that could go to bed easily with unfinished problems with someone I loved. But I knew I was being taken for granted.

As I continued to close my wallet, Nick became more irritated with me. Nick started saying he hated me being on Only Fans. Now, after a year, Only Fans was an issue. It was never an issue when I was paying for everything and when he would text me every day about how he wanted us to get rich. I toned down my Only Fans content to make him happy, because although I knew it wasn't a genuine issue for him, I tried hard to make it seem like I valued his opinion. We were in Arizona on a trip I had booked for us a while back so he could golf with his friends. I paid a lot of money for this weekend getaway. We went to a nice restaurant with my sister, and as Nick went to the restroom, I vented to my sister about it. Caley and I were extremely close, we talked every day. She was well aware of the shit he was doing to me. When he got back to the table, the bill came. He just sat there and continued to sip his whiskey. "Hey babe." I said to him. "I am super stressed about money, I have toned down my only fans and I want to delete it one day, and this trip has cost me two thousand dollars for our flights, and Airbnb." I made it seem like I was now struggling. I kind of was. I had spent money like it was going out of style, I was stupid. And my own boyfriend was taking advantage of me. "Alright. I'll pay for dinner." He replied, irritated.

We got back to our Airbnb, and we were both having some wine when he said, "You've changed." He wasn't wrong but this wasn't the time or place to talk about it. "Uh… yeah I have Nick." I said nervously, but honestly. "Yep. I fucking knew it. You're trying to act like you pay for everything. I have more money than you." He yelled. He really yelled this. I was taken back by it because was no leading up to this shout from him. He was already at one hundred. "You have more money than me? Of course you do! I pay for literally fucking everything! And for your kids. It's bullshit Nick." I shouted. This time, I did shout back. I was at my breaking point. Nick stormed in the kitchen and said, "You're so fucking shallow and vapid and ungrateful. God I just want to dump this fucking water on you." That's when I felt scared, if he was going so mad to the point where he was going to pour water on me, then that's where it ends with me. I sat up off the couch and said, "You need to leave." Calmly. I was so calm for some reason I just collected my emotions and knew this was a relationship with zero respect anymore. I was texting my sister who lived nearby letting her know what was happening. Nick's brother and friends were staying in Arizona too for the golf weekend, so I knew he could go there. I shut and locked the bedroom door and waited for him to leave. He continued to yell outside the door calling me names. My mom has called me enough names in this world to last me a lifetime. They didn't hurt me, but once a relationship gets to name calling, it's over for me. As I heard him roll his suitcase towards the front door, I heard a loud "BANG!" I walked over and opened the bedroom door and saw glass shattered all over the place and a huge dent in the bedroom door. There was wine all over the white rug. I looked at him and said, "You need to leave, or I will call the cops." I said it so softly he knew I was serious. He slammed the front door and left.

I cleaned up the glass and cried nonstop. I'll be damned if I am cleaning up broken glass after a forty-year-old man. I won't do this; this is the type of shit my mom and Jake would do. I refuse to have a relationship like hers was. I had more respect for myself than that, I had more respect for my son to let a guy like this around either of us. I ended up calling Kyle. I got his voicemail, and I cried as I said, "I am so sorry, and I understand if you hate me, but I am done with him and I miss you and want to be with you." I called my brother Tyler and told him what happened, and I needed to fix this dent in the door. I didn't want to be fined as a renter and get a bad review on my Airbnb profile. I ended up booking my brother a flight out to Arizona at five in the morning and having him help me. We had to buy a new door, paint, tools, and stain remover for the rug. Caley and Tyler, both helped me, and we were able to fix all the damages. Meanwhile, Nick was texting me telling me he was sorry, and that he loved me and hated fighting with me. I didn't care, this trip went from two thousand, to three thousand dollars just to pay for the damages and to fly my brother out. Nick said he would pay for the damages and sent me only three hundred and fifty dollars. This didn't even scratch the surface of what I had pay for. When I told him what everything actually cost, he wasn't willing to cover the damages any further. But wanted to prove to me that he would be better. He admitted to being insecure about many things, and with my TV show coming out, and my social media following, it made him worried that I was going to leave him for someone famous. He even told me he would stop drinking. I didn't care, the damage was done and beyond repair. I couldn't proceed with a relationship where there was name calling, broken glass, and threatening to throw water on me now. I did not get an entire divorce with my son's father, live completely broke with my toxic mother, just to be in a relationship with a narcissist. I was done.

Chapter Thirty- Five

Weeks went by as I slowly but surely picked up the pieces after ending things with Nick. I felt so incredibly strong because this was the first time, I had ended a relationship while I still loved him. Any other relationship, I had fallen out of love before ending it and this was hard, but my son mattered most, and I refused to let my son be potentially exposed to this type of relationship. Although he never saw us fight, I know how these things work, the abuser gets more comfortable, and they no longer care about their audience.

I continued to see and talk to Kyle. He was so kind, and never once used it against me what stupid decisions I had made in this past year. I decided to tell him about Only Fans. I wanted to be honest, and he deserved that. If he truly loved me then he would see me and love me for me. I told him all about it and how it started. He looked at me and said, "I appreciate you for being honest, and although I don't love that the girl I like has photos out there for other guys to look at, I understand why you made it and respect that if helped you and Bentley." I melted in that moment. He was so understanding, didn't judge me, and still wanted to be with me. At the time, I would only let him come see me on the days I didn't have Bentley. He would ask to come and see me other days, but if I had Bentley, I would tell him he couldn't yet. Eventually he said, "Are you ever going to let me meet him?" and I said, "One day." One morning, Kyle was at my house, and we started to talk about making things official. I sat on his lap and looked at him and said, "I don't want to pressure you Kyle, but if we do this, and we decide to be official, then that means you understand I have my son, and when I am ready for you to meet him, that is a big deal. And I don't just want some temporary guy around him. So let me know if you want to be officially together, or we can just see each other on the days I don't have him, but I don't want you to meet him unless we are serious." Kyle looked at me while playing with my hair and said, "Candi, I am sure I am serious about you. I have pursued you for two years, I've always wanted you. And when you are comfortable and ready for me to meet Bentley, then I am excited." It was as if everything in the world went silent and it was only him and I. I smiled the warmest smile I have ever felt since giving birth to Bentley, and leaned in and kissed him.

My relationship with Kyle was beyond easy. He is the most amazing man I have ever met. He met Bentley for the first time and Kyle was amazing with him. I took Bentley to see Kyle after we rode horses for the day with my stepsister Jenny. Kyle was at work so Bentley was able to sit in the cop car and put on Kyle's SWAT vest which weighed almost as much as he did. My heart was so full. Kyle treats me as if I am the most beautiful woman in the world. There are never any trust issues, and after being together for well over a year, we have never had a fight. I have been open with him about how my mom is and have often called him crying when she would pick a fight with me. It was so embarrassing to share with him how my mom really is, and it took some time. Kyle comes from a healthy family; his parents are still married, and he and his brother are both very hard-working men in law enforcement. So, you could imagine my embarrassment when I would finally open up to him, however, he never made me feel as if I should be embarrassed. He would let me cry, and vent, and then help me to regroup by reassuring me that I am a good person, I am a good mom, and it will be okay.

Kyle is always so grounded, and strong minded, yet the most tender man when it comes to me. The way Kyle touches and holds me is with absolute love and intention. I've never felt anything like this in my life. This big strong man, that makes me feel safe, and respected every single day. Kyle is opposite of me, I am loud, dramatic, emotional, love to dance, social media poster, reality TV binger, and soon to star on a reality TV show. And Kyle is quiet, reserved, composed, hates social media and reality TV, but is the absolute most supportive man of my career and hobbies. I, for the first time in my life, am incredibly inspired by the man I am with. The communication is always healthy and effective, our sex life is beyond perfect, and he is so good to Bentley. I thank God every single day for him.

My mom was happy for me at first, but then started to get sick of me telling people about how amazing he is when people would ask about him. Not that I would overly brag because I knew how much she would hate that. But even if I said, "He is the most amazing man I've ever met." My mom would just roll her eyes. One afternoon, my mom and her friend and I decided to go to a cute little wine bar downtown. I curled my hair and dressed in the cute yet casual outfit. As we walked into the wine bar, this girl who seemed happy and tipsy came up to me and said, "You are so cute! Oh my god you are adorable!" She was so sweet and complimented me as we walked in. "Thank you love." I said with appreciation, my mom rolled her eyes. "Ugh really." My mom smirked. "What?" I said. "Really Candi? She's a fucking bitch, she just compliments you and neither of us, as we're just standing here?" She barked. "God, mom she was just complimenting." I said. "No, it's fucking rude Candi." She spoke. I just got quiet, hoping that girl didn't come up to say anything further as we sat at our table because I knew my mom wasn't afraid to be rude to her.

I found myself often being worried if someone was going to compliment me at any time when would go places with my mom because I knew it would bother her. If someone commented my hair, my mom would say, "She can thank me for that." Yes, my mom had amazing hair, that yes, genetically I was lucky enough to have, but I wasn't allowed to accept or take ownership of the compliment if it was given by a stranger when she was around.

My mom was more of a "friend" than a mom. Although, I would never be friends with someone like her. We would have dinner together often, and not all nights were bad. I was grateful for those nights. Having Bentley was such a blessing because my mom truly adores him and is an excellent grandmother. But she started to get more comfortable fighting with me in front of him, and that's when I started to try and shield things. I would try and add healthy quality time with my mom. I convinced her to come to spin class with me, and once she started to enjoy it, I bought her these expensive spin shoes in her favorite color to encourage us to go more often. Getting my mom into working out was beautiful. It felt so much better for us to spend time together when it involved something healthy. I wanted her to get her confidence back, and a healthy lifestyle, which in turn equates to a healthy mindset.

My mom's birthday was approaching when I decided to get her a special gift, there was this famous medium who could talk to past loved ones. I spent over seven hundred dollars on this appointment and the medium was hard to get an appointment with. My mom's birthday was beginning of August, and I was able to get her an appointment just a couple weeks after that. I submitted a few photos of my mom's mom to the medium hoping that during my mom's appointment, she could connect with her mom. I felt like this would be just what my mom needed, she was clearly so angry and hurting inside, so I felt like this could be so healing for her if she could potentially hear from her mom. When I told my mom to make sure her schedule was clear for this specific day and why, she was skeptical and hesitant.  She didn't like to believe in that sort of thing, and never did I really until I really watched this medium's work and I felt this could be so amazing if there was some sort of sign that her mom was here for her. I knew my mom needed it, whether she was too proud to admit it or not. As we approached the day of my mom's appointment, my mom realized that the appointment wasn't until next year. This medium was so booked up, that I secured an appointment not even realizing that's how far out she was booked. I apologized to my mom, as she truly knew this was an honest mistake, but I was still excited for the upcoming appointment, even if it was still a year out. If anything, this made me admire the medium even more considering she was in such high demand. "So, what are you getting me for my birthday this year?" my mom said. "Well mom, I booked that psychic medium appointment for you." I uncomfortably pointed out. "That is next year's gift, where is my 'this year's' gift?" She said. She tried to make it sarcastic, but she was serious. Ever since I started making a little more money, I would spoil her. Facials, massages, dinners, beauty enhancements, and I even lent her money once when she needed it. She felt like my money was her money in a sense.

I am angry with myself as far as how overly generous I was with treating the people I love financially. I started to notice my mom would hardly reach for her wallet anymore at dinner. I had created a monster. When my sister came to town one time, who is a successful nurse and still gets help financially between Jed and my mom. We all went to lunch, it was my mom, Caley, myself, and Bentley. We finished our meals, when the bill came, my mom looked at me and said, "Wanna split it?" I replied in a snarky way, "Um, okay I'm the single mom, and Caley is the nurse." I refrained from pointing out the fact that her bills were always going to be paid, but I felt like me being a single mom was legitimate enough. "She's visiting." My mom said. I was so irritated with her, it wouldn't matter if I was visiting from out of town, my mom would make sure I paid for my share regardless. I had spent so much money on my ex, and so much money on my own mom, that I wasn't making money like I used to. Not to mention, the taxes I was paying on top of that. What was the point of making more money, when they take enough to make sure you feel broke and depressed all over again.

Don't' get me wrong, I am grateful that my sister and I experienced a different mom. Our mom had her moments often with anyone, but I knew a different side of mom. Although she was always confrontational and an unpredictable time bomb, the monster I knew inside her, was something I was glad no one else had to witness. As hurt and as sensitive I am, I knew I was always going to survive.

## Chapter Thirty- Six

I had just gotten done hosting a charity event and raising money for the American Heart Association. I was able to exceed my goal of raising over one thousand dollars for the organization. I felt so fulfilled by using my platform to give back and my biggest passion was to help the fight against human trafficking. I enjoyed the feeling of being some sort of help or support for charity. After the American Heart association event, I gave Bentley a bath. We always had this funny routine where after the bath, he would run around the house naked as I chased him and tried to get his boxers on him. I would chase him, and Cora did too. She would get so excited right as he got out of the bath, she knew what time it was, and she was very vocal about it. This was our nightly routine and Bentley would just laugh and laugh. On this night, were started our chase when I notice Cora slightly coughed twice while she was running. I stopped mid run, practically froze, and I have no idea what came over me, but I stopped and said, "Her heart." And overwhelming voice in my head. Every muscle in my body told me something was wrong with her heart. I can't really explain it, but it was like God, or an Angel came to tell me what it was.

Cora was fine after that night. She was eating, drinking, playing, not acting weird, playing in the snow with me for the following four days. One morning, I woke up and looked beside me to say good morning to Cora like I do every morning. She never left my side; she was always in her dog bed next to me and this morning she wasn't there. I walked into the living room to find her, she was on her dog bed in the living room and breathing differently. I sat with her, "Are you okay Cora Jo?" I said, concerned. This wasn't her; this wasn't my Cora. I took her to the emergency vet, they have you wait in your car while they take your dog in, and then they call you with the Doctor's findings. This gives you a chance to approve any medical care, and if you have time to leave for the day so they can call you when it's time to come pick up your pet. As I waited in my car nervously waiting to hear the initial assessment, they called me, "Candi? Hi, the Doctor wants you to come in and talk to you for a minute." "Okay…" I said. I knew this was bad. They don't usually do this. I sat in this room and started to tear up, I wasn't with Cora in this room, I just waited. The vert finally came in and said, "Candi, what do you think is going on with Cora?" I looked up at him and said, "I want you to tell me she has an ear infection. But I think it's her heart." As I broke down in tears, hardly finishing my own sentence. Saying it out loud hurt so much because deep down I knew and didn't want to admit it. "Yes, it is her heart, Candi. She has a tumor in her heart, there is fluid around her heart, and there is no cure. It is life threatening." The Vet said. He was compassionate, but very matter of fact which I needed. I broke down, completely. They brought Cora in with me so I could spend some time with her. I sat on the floor with her and cried to her and hugged her. She was disoriented and she wasn't even on medication yet. Her body was shutting down, and fast. I hated seeing her like that, but now I see I needed to see her like that to remind myself there was no alternative and I took her in at the right time. I stayed with her as it was time to put her to sleep. I had such PTSD from the time I put JoJo down I was starting to panic inside but held it in. I laid with Cora and stroked her head the whole time saying, "You're such a good girl, you're such a good girl Cora Jo, I love you." I didn't even know she was gone. It was the most peaceful thing I have ever seen; she didn't even show a struggle, it was like she completely went to sleep. I laid with her and kissed her and kissed her over and over telling her I loved her. I wasn't expecting to have to say goodbye to my best friend that day. I was never going to be the same again.

I called Kyle crying, and he knew how much I was hurting. Kyle was stuck in SWAT training and couldn't leave to come be with me. To be honest, I didn't want him to. I was a mess, ugly crying, on my bathroom floor. I needed to let it out for a bit. I was, however, grateful my mom came to be with me. She stayed with me for two nights. In a way, I realized I needed the company no matter who it was, because anytime I was alone, I would lose it. Even if my mom went to the bathroom, I'd break down. I couldn't be alone, and Bentley was at his dad's that weekend, which I think was a good thing because I didn't want him to see Cora like that, and then to see me like I was. I truly feel that God works in mysterious ways. My mom sat next to me on the cough as we turned on a movie. I had looked up a canvas printing website to order nice quality canvas prints of Cora, myself, and Bentley. I leaned over and showed my mom the three photos I chose to be printed and shipped to me. "Don't overdo it, Candi." My mom said. "Mom, I miss her." Is all I could say without getting choked up. I felt a lump in my throat. She completely cut me down and made me feel as if I was being ridiculous by ordering photos of my dog which I had lost just less than twenty-four hours ago. It hurt, and not to mention, this was my money, my house, and my dog. I don't expect everyone to understand the bond between a pet and an owner, but if you see someone who is completely shattered by losing their pet, and they want to order a couple pictures in remembrance of them, I would support that without question.

A couple of weeks went by and not a single day without crying. Bentley took the news well, I decided to tell him on the phone the day it happened. I figured it would be best that he processed it while he was at his dad's instead of waiting for him to come home and to be blindsided with the new emptiness in our home. I was trying so hard to hold my tears in when Bentley was home. One of my friends reached out to me to check on me. "Hey you, how are you doing? I know it's hard Candi, but Cora is always with you." My friend said. I replied and said, "I'm hanging in there. I am just sad because everyone tells me I will get signs from her, or dream about her and I haven't. I am sad she is mad at me or feels like I gave up on her." "She doesn't feel that way Candi. She was telling you it was her time. She will give you a sign." She replied. "I just feel so alone." I said. I was exhausted, and drained. I let Bentley sleep with me that night. I fell asleep rather quickly after sending that last message to my friend. I was in a deep sleep, when something woke me up. I opened my eyes out of a dead sleep and saw this light blue glowing figure slowly floating down toward Bentley and me. I felt so calm, so still, so comfortable. I watched this beautiful glowing orb make its way closer as I watched with ease. I felt this overwhelming feeling of warmth and love when it finally reached my comforter and disappeared in between Bentley and me. As I started to recollect myself and tried to process what that was, I grabbed my phone. I immediately looked up what this blue, glowing, orb meant. The exact words of "If you see a blue glowing orb, this is a loved one coming to reassure you that you are not alone." I cried and cried the happiest tears ever. I was flooded with heavy yet beautiful emotions. I have never felt something so powerful in my life. I needed this, Cora is still with me, and I miss her every single day.

My dad was coming up from Napa with my stepmom Sherry. They usually come up every few months to see Bentley and me. We always go to dinner at the same place and request our favorite server. My dad and Sherry have a lot of friends and they all like to come up to as well. They make a big trip out of it and stay at their favorite casino with their friends, they gamble and love to have a good time. Bentley was with his dad that weekend however, so I had invited one of my friends to join us since she was going to be in town and wanted to see me. I met my mom for spin class that morning when she asked, "What are you doing tonight?" "My dad is coming up with Sherry and some of their friends, so I am going to meet them for dinner." I replied. "What friends?" my mom asked. "I can't remember all their names, but one guy is Peter from Boston, and another guy named Dax or something. I can't remember, but they're all really cool." I said. My mom's face lit up when I mentioned two male names. "Well, you should invite me." She said. I was a little taken back by it. Honestly waiting for her to almost say she was kidding. I paused, as she looked at me with an even harder stare and jerked her head signaling for me to answer her. "Um, Mom. You can't just invite yourself to dinner…" I said. She instantly got upset. She gave me the cold shoulder and stormed out after spin class not saying a word. She was used to me texting or calling her trying to explain myself further so she would have an excuse to be cruel and make me feel like shit. I was done, I was checked out. I had just lost my dog and she was pulling this? I was done catering to her antics. She always knew I would come crawling back her, and this time was absurd. My dad and Sherry are the kindest people and most welcoming people ever. They would have been fine with it if I had invited my mom to tag along, but it's not my place to hook my mom up with my dad's friends. It's wildly inappropriate and not my place. I couldn't believe she was genuinely mad I didn't let her come to dinner with her ex-husband. Spending time with my dad and Sherry is a totally different experience. I am used to any and almost all quality time waiting for an explosion. My dad and Sherry can have dinner, cocktails, and laugh and that's how simple it is. There have been times I have invited my sister Caley to join us for dinner and my dad and Sherry treat her like their own. So welcoming and so enjoyable to be around. Even Caley mentioned how nice it is to see how this is how family time should be. Therefore, I'll be damned if I was going to invite my mom, with alcohol, and feel on edge the entire night.

I was getting ready for dinner with my dad and went on a live stream on my social media platform. It's something I do often to engage with my followers and it also makes money at times. I was curling my hair, waiting for my friend to get to my house. Everyone on live asked what I was up to. "My friend is about to be here, and we are going to meet my dad, stepmom, and their friends for a drink and then dinner." I said. I was in a giddy mood to be honest. It was the first time I had really smiled much since losing Cora. I think it was because I was getting out of the house, and knew I was going to be in good company. My mom apparently was watching the live and sent me a text saying, "Wow." I looked at my phone while on the live and my face dropped. She knew was she was doing. She was trying to make me feel like a jerk for inviting a friend and not her, and she wanted to see my reaction on live. She would have waited until after the live to text me this if she didn't enjoy making me feel like I needed to explain myself. I was so done with this. I was not going to have her gaslight me and make me out to be the bad guy because I had invited a friend to dinner with my dad and not her. Not to mention, my friend wasn't going to meet my dad's friends. Even if they didn't have friends joining us, it still isn't weird to bring my friend with me, but it is weird to bring my dad's ex-wife uninvited. I was stunned as I read the text. It was obvious on the livestream that my energy just dropped. I held my phone as I looked at the iPad, I was doing the live on, and almost didn't know how to respond. I text her back saying, "Mom, I had invited my friend a day earlier and it's not wrong for me to invite my friend to dinner with my dad and Sherry." My mom replied, "I don't need you in my life." That right there was all I needed to finally say, "Fuck it." I looked at everyone on camera, and I didn't hold back. This was the first time I had decided to stop protecting the person who purposely hurts me. I told everyone on live what I was dealing with, and I didn't care. People will so easily say to leave their family drama off the internet. But the thing is, I have been so open about my life, my struggles, my divorce on the internet and that's what has grown my following because people and relate and appreciate my authenticity. I don't sugarcoat things; I am very open and honest. This is how I was sought out by producers to be on a TV show. But the one thing I never shared with my followers, was about my childhood. My mom would already get angry when I said I was the "black sheep" of the family. I protected her so much and kept my mouth shut. This time I was done, I don't care anymore. I lost Cora, she knew the pain I was feeling, and she once again made this about herself. I don't need this anymore.

I met my dad for dinner, and it was a great time. My dad bought a book for me to read to Bentley. It was a children's book about losing a pet. When Bentley was back with me, we laid in bed as I started to read the book to him. It was about a boy losing his dog, his best friend, his everything, and the dog's name was JoJo. I had chills, and started to cry as I knew this was such a sign. My dad didn't even know the book had a dog named JoJo in it. My first German Shepherd JoJo was my first dog, the first thing that was absolutely mine, and so loyal to me. Years later when Cora came into my life, I knew it was JoJo within her. Everyone who knew me well would joke and say, "Your last dog is the exact same. It's got to be your parenting." It was a running joke for years because both of my German Shepherds were so much alike. They were the most girly, prissy, German Shepherds they could've passed at cats. This book was an absolute sign. JoJo was nine years old and passed away in March, Cora Jo was nine years old and also passed away in March.

A couple days went by when I finally broke down crying. Bentley was with his dad, and I was alone. I missed my son and Cora, and I had this sadness about my mom. She was always an easy distraction when I needed it. Although not a positive one. I was sad, and angry that I couldn't have even avoided this fight between us. And if I had invited her to dinner, I am sure something else would have happened. But me inviting her to dinner when I didn't want to because it was unnecessary, would be me, once again, catering to her selfish wants. I spent the whole day crying. I didn't even shower until late that night. I was hurting. The next day I finally got back on a livestream. Everyone had asked me how the rest of my night when considering they saw me end the last livestream very upset. I explained on live how I was feeling and how I finally felt about my mom. I didn't care anymore, protecting her reputation didn't serve me any peace. I had found a quote that said, "If it was a lie that holds you captive, then it is the truth that will set you free." This resonated with me heavily. As I was venting on my livestream, I saw a comment that someone said, "How about you talk about your stepdad and the allegations against him and why your mom left him." "What?" I said, this was obviously someone that knew me, but clearly didn't know the facts. Come to find out, it was my uncle Mark, my mom's brother. I got a text message from him saying, "I am done with you." I ended the live immediately in tears. I called him twice, and no answer. My cousin called me and said, "What happened? My dad is so upset with you, he said he saw you bashing your mom online." "I wasn't bashing her, I was venting, but where is the lie? I said what I said. And meant it. I am done holding back." I said. I further explained that all this stemmed from me not inviting her to dinner with my dad. My cousin was shocked to find that out this is what started this feud. My cousin told me she was going to talk to her dad and explain further and call me later. I cried for hours; this was ridiculous. When my cousin called me back she said my uncle and my mom are both infuriated with me and that they three way called her to talk all about me. My cousin explained why her dad left that comment on my livestream, and said, "Candi, this makes me uncomfortable to say this to you, but my dad said that comment today because your mom left Jed because he was molesting you." "What!" I screamed, "What! That is so far from the fucking truth. Are you kidding me? My stepdad was physically violent with me, but that man never touched me sexually, ever." I was shaking. This didn't even make sense because my stepdad never sexually assaulted me, and even when he was physically abusive, my mom didn't leave him at all! She stayed with him the entire time, I was living in Los Angeles with my boyfriend at the time and they were still together. My mom and Jed split because he cheated on her, not because of any form of abuse. I explained all this to my cousin while shaking with anger. "Maybe Uncle Mark has the story mixed up. My mom told me my dad molested me. Maybe uncle Mark thought it was Jed." I said. My cousin told me she didn't think he messed up the story at all. I started to unwind. If my dad had molested me, then why the fuck would she want to go to dinner with him? If Jed molested me, why wouldn't she have said this about him when she was publicly bashing him all over the internet, saying anything she could to slander his name when he was fighting for custody. Nothing made sense anymore. The only thing I knew for sure. Is that my mom is a fucking liar, a complete liar. I text my sister, because if she knew our mom made such a sick allegation about her own dad, she would be livid. When I told her, she was furious. Caley text my mom asking if this was true that she said this when my mom told her no, that was about my real dad. But then had told Caley that I was molested at a Daycare when I was younger. What the fuck was wrong with her. Nothing added up, she was lying so poorly that it validated how much I hated her now.

I received a text message from my mom saying, "You better cancel that appointment with the Medium or I will. And you're going to apologize to me, and you better make it public." "Fuck her." I said out loud as I read it. First of all, she told me to cancel the medium appointment I got her because she knew how sentimental it was for me to get her a session with the medium, not because she wasn't into it. And two, I owe her an apology? No, I am no longer your punching bag mommy dearest.

## Chapter Thirty-Seven

As hard as this last month has been, I feel that everything happens for a reason. I cry every single day missing Cora. But I thank God for how he made it happen. She didn't suffer, she wasn't in pain, she told me quickly it was her time. I thank God for making sure Bentley wasn't with me at the time she had passed, I thank God for giving me a sign a few days prior something was going on with her heart. I thank God for sending her to give me a sign that she is always with me. I thank God for showing me at my most fragile time that my mom is not a positive presence in my life. That may sound cold, but many people have this misconception that you must have this undying loyalty to someone because they are "family." I find this to be the most toxic perspective in the world. Just because someone gave birth to you or is your family member does not give them a hall pass to hurt you. You are not a punching bag, and you were not put on this earth to allow someone to bring you pain. Many people ask me how with my social media platforms, how I handle the "trolls" and the negative comments. It's simple, not one stranger who doesn't personally know me can hurt my feelings with their opinions about me. The only people who can and have hurt me, are the ones I loved. The person I strived for comfort, trust, and protection from, has betrayed me the most, therefore it has made me untouchable to a stranger. I thank God for it all.

I do not sit at home crying over how I wish my mom was different. I don't wish that at all, and I never will. I always say, "You can't miss what you never had." I am beyond grateful that my mom was the way that she was. I needed this childhood; it has made me who

I am today. It made me the mother I am today. I am beyond proud of myself for the mommy I am to Bentley. Every single day, I tell Bentley how proud I am of him, how smart he is, how funny he is, and how lucky I am to be his mommy. I look at my son and my heart is so full, I have never loved anyone so much in my life and I would die for him. I will protect my son, I will be there to guide him, to lift him, and love him endlessly. I will never understand how a every mother couldn't feel this way about their child.

The type of girlfriend or partner I am to my boyfriend today is something I thoroughly enjoy being. I have never loved, and respected someone so much, and I feel this in return. Kyle is a man I look up to, and I have never looked up to a man before. His mindset is inspiring, he is in control of his emotions, he is caring, he is loving, he is compassionate, and loyal. When he touches me, he touches me with love. He lets me be me without judging me, he is proud of me and supportive. Bentley loves him and I am beyond proud that my son witnesses what love is supposed to look like. He sees us hold hands, he us interact, and that is exactly the type of man I want my son to be to his girlfriend or wife one day.

The woman I am today, is a woman I am very proud of. I am not perfect, I am growing, and I am constantly inspired by influential people daily. I have my flaws, I am quick to react, often sometimes stoop to a lower level when defending myself, but I will never hurt anyone first. I love whole heartedly, so if I am attacked, I become a bull charging the red flag, however this is where I am accountable. I strive to be better than that. One thing I will always be is accountable. If I make a mistake, I will own it. I thank God for any and all mistakes I have made because he has shown me to learn from them. I have a very forgiving heart and go out of my way to make people feel better. I can't stand it if I know someone is struggling, I will go out of my way to give my support and try to lift anyone's spirits. I have privately sent single mother's money, I donate to my local animal shelter, and continue to donate and raise awareness for human trafficking. God put me on this earth for a reason, and I feel that I am finally realizing what it is. I never knew that my presence, and my authenticity on my social media platform would turn in to what it is. I have had so many women reach out to me thanking me for making them laugh, for giving them confidence, and for showing them it's okay to stand up for yourself. I don't do this for followers, for fame, or for money, I do this because it feels good. It feels good to make other's feel good. I know what it's like to feel broken, helpless, defeated, and unloved. And if any of you can relate to those negative thoughts, I am here to remind you that you are strong, you are resilient, and you have survived one hundred percent of your bad days. If you stay true to yourself, and move forward with a pure heart, God, The Universe, or whatever it is you may believe in, will not let you down. You will not fail if you love yourself and have good intentions.

Divorce does not define you. I will always say that a happy mom is a good mom. You are not selfish for choosing peace, for choosing love, and for setting boundaries. These are strong words that apply to any kind of relationship. Whether it is relationships, work, friends, or family, you are not a bad person for protecting your peace. When I think about my mom, I am grateful she has given me a place to stay when I needed it, but everything has always been conditional. To this day, I despise gifts, I won't allow anyone to do a favor for me because I am used to it being thrown back in my face. I have created a life that no one can compromise for my son and me. There is not one person who can take credit for giving me the life I have today but me.

Writing this book has been very challenging for me. I have always kept the truth of my childhood a secret, or somewhat lighthearted. I will no longer protect the person who never protected me. I want to make it clear that this is not to punish, bash, or shame my mother. This is my story, this is my truth, this is why I am the way that I am. I am sure my mom did the best she could to the best of her capability. I
am grateful that she was a different mom for my little brother and sister. My mom harbors a lot of anger, and resentment for some reason, and I have finally come to a point where I realize it is not my job to cater to her trauma. She is a wonderful grandmother to Bentley, and she loves him dearly. If she were to ask to see him and spend a day with him, I would absolutely allow it. I refuse to use my son as a pawn. I strongly dislike the saying, "You must respect your elders." I call bullshit, if you do bad things to innocent people, you do not get my respect. I don't care what age, blood relative or not, if you hurt people, you lose people. I love my mom, and I wish her nothing but the best, but I need to protect myself now. And I will always remember, God

brought me to it, and he will get me through it. We are all a work in progress, and no matter what age, I truly think people can heal and change with the right mindset, but you can not exhaust yourself trying to change people into becoming a better person. I am a woman of strength, I am a woman of desire, and I am a woman love. When I was little, I took on so much that wasn't mine to carry, this is where I set it down. It takes a great deal of healing to realize that narcissists don't want what is best for their children, they want what is convenient for themselves. I am celebrating myself loudly this year, and I don't care if nobody claps for me or not, I know God is.

Another thing to remember is that not everyone that hurts your feelings, cares. Read that again. Not everyone that hurts your feelings, cares. You need to let that idea go that you need "closure." You don't always get closure by someone who hurt you, because not all apologies are sincere, and some are non-existent. Closure is you, picking up the pieces and moving forward with faith, and love. Hurt people often hurt people, but not all do. I have been hurt but would never want my son or any child to endure the same. My life, my trauma, my childhood wasn't the worst, there are many people who have suffered beyond our imagination, but this is my life. This is me releasing the chains, and moving forward with the life I was given by God. It is helpful to understand acceptance. Once you accept that you cannot change people to do better, and accept that your journey is yours, and their journey is theirs, it will bring you a great deal of peace. Sometimes God brings people into your life who aren't meant to stay there forever. Your light in this world is always going to irritate the wrong people, pay attention to this and be okay with setting the boundaries that you deserve to set in place. Remember, a happy mom is a good mom.

Made in United States
North Haven, CT
24 May 2023